Praise for *The Stephensons' Rocket*

Winner of a Writing for Children award in the Winchester Writers' Conference: 'a clear, strong first person narrative, with great immediacy ... the humour is lovely.'

Jude Evans, Little Tiger Press

'A great read – you won't be able to put it down!'
Sandra Horn, award-winning children's author

'A delightful book that deserves to be widely read. The perfect gift for our younger supporters.'
The Retired Greyhound Trust

D0434530

Jayne Woodhouse has written many non-fiction books and curriculum resources for children and schools. Her publishers include BBC Active, Ginn, Heinemann, Longman and PCET. She has also been a primary school teacher and teacher trainer.

She lives in Southampton with her daughter. This is her first novel.

The Stephensons' Rocket

Jayne Woodhouse

The Clucket Press

The Stephensons' Rocket

First published in the UK 2009 by The Clucket Press

Typeset by Niall Horn, The Clucket Press

Printed and bound in the UK by Athenaeum Press Ltd, Gateshead, Tyne and Wear NE11 0PZ

British Library Cataloguing in Publication Data
A CIP catalogue record for this book is available from the British Library

ISBN-13: 978-0-9549256-7-3

The Clucket Press
220 Hill Lane, Southampton, Hants SO15 7NR

www.tattybogle.com

For Josian, with love

And in fond memory of another Rocky:

dog of kings; king of dogs

CHAPTER 1

It was three o'clock on Saturday afternoon, and Dad still wasn't back from the pub. Mum scraped his meat pie into a dish and flung it in the fridge. Then she banged all the cupboard doors as she cleared away.

My brother Darren was fed up with waiting. 'Dad promised me we'd play football this afternoon,' he moaned. 'He never keeps his promises! It's not fair!'

We all know that, so I don't understand why Darren still gets upset. It's because he's only ten, I suppose. I'm eleven, so I've had longer to get used to it. Dad had promised to take me swimming as well, but I didn't even bother to mention it.

'It's no use whining to me, Darren,' Mum snapped at him, 'go and have a kickabout with Anna.'

'We can go up the park,' I said, trying to sound like I meant it.

'Don't be stupid!' shouted Darren. 'I don't want to play football with a girl!' He stormed off, stamped

1

upstairs and slammed his bedroom door.

'I'd better get on with my homework,' I said, hurrying up to my room as well.

It was a good excuse to keep out of Mum's way. Besides, I knew Dad was in big trouble again and I didn't want to be around when he turned up.

Finally, I heard Dad's key in the lock. Mum ran straight to the front door, like she couldn't wait to have a good shout.

'Wherever have you been?' I could hear her yelling at him. 'And what on earth are you doing with that thing?'

'Sorry I'm late, Jo, but the kids are going to love this!' Dad sounded very cheerful. 'Anna! Darren! I've got something to show you!'

'What is it?' I called, although it was hard to be interested. Things Dad brought home were always useless, like the bike with odd wheels or the skateboard that didn't have any.

'It's a dog!'

A dog! I'd only been wanting a dog for nearly forever! Even Darren was excited enough to forget about sulking, because he came rushing down the stairs right behind me.

But this wasn't the cuddly puppy I'd imagined. Leaning up against Dad was a tall, bony creature, on legs so long and thin they looked like they could snap as easily as twigs.

'That's not a dog!' grumbled Darren. 'It's a rat on stilts!'

'Shut up Darren!' I hissed.

Darren was being horrible, but secretly I thought he wasn't far wrong. Still, it explained where Dad had been all this time. He must have found this poor animal abandoned somewhere and been trying to help it.

'It's all right, you're safe now,' I said gently to the dog and went to stroke him.

But Mum pulled me back. 'Don't you dare touch it, Anna! It might bite!'

Dad took no notice. 'I want you all to meet someone very special,' he announced proudly. 'Say hello to Sheldon Rocket, but you can call him Rocky!'

It seemed like a fancy name for an old stray dog. And however did Dad know what he was called? That's when I realised Dad was up to something again – and I knew it wouldn't be good.

'Rocky's a racing greyhound!' Dad announced, beaming all over his face.

'A racing greyhound?' repeated Mum, in amazement.

I couldn't believe it either.

'That's right! Isn't he a beauty?' Dad replied.

Rocky had a dirty, matted coat that looked like it had once been white. One front leg was black, as if he was wearing a long, odd sock and there was a matching black patch over his right eye. He was trembling all over.

'He's a bit skinny,' was all I could think of to say.

'That's because Rocky's an athlete,' said Dad, 'he's built for speed. Go on, Jo, let the girl stroke him.'

I patted the dog gently on the head. I could feel his skull under the skin. I didn't want to stroke the rest of him, because I couldn't bear to feel those sticking-out bones. Rocky looked at me for a moment with big, wet eyes, then dropped his head again.

'He looks ever so nervous,' said Darren.

'That's because he's highly strung,' explained Dad patiently.

'Well, you're not coming inside with that thing,' snapped Mum. 'It's filthy and it stinks!'

'*It* happens to be a pedigree animal,' said Dad, 'I've got a certificate to prove it. And he's fast – you should see him go! He's not called The Rocket for nothing.'

'You've seen him run then, have you?' Mum was using her ever-so-patient voice, which meant she was absolutely furious.

'Not exactly,' Dad admitted, 'but I've seen his potential.'

'So you're telling me this skeleton is a prize-winning greyhound?' Mum asked.

'This dog is the passport to the Stephensons' future success!' Dad replied. 'He just needs a bit of training up – then we take him down the dog track, put a few quid on him and make a fortune!'

And that's when Mum hit on the very worst part. 'You didn't pay any money for this animal did you, Pete?' she said, much too quietly.

'Now come on, Jo, you can't get a champion dog like this for free!'

'You did, didn't you?' Mum exploded. 'You actually paid money for this thing! How much? How much did it cost you?'

'Only a hundred quid!' Dad actually sounded delighted. 'Can you believe it, he only cost me a hundred quid – Sheldon Rocket, the Champion of Champions!'

'Pete Stephenson, the Idiot of Idiots, more like!' Mum was white with rage. 'Who on earth would sell a prize greyhound for a hundred pounds? They're worth thousands! You're telling me you threw all that money away on this flea-bitten mongrel?'

'Mum,' I thought I'd better try interrupting, 'I think he's thirsty!'

'Your dad's always thirsty,' snapped Mum, 'that's why he's forever down the pub.'

'No, Mum, I mean the dog. I think he needs a drink.'

Rocky's tongue was hanging right out like a long, pink rug and you could hear him panting.

'Good girl, Anna. Go and fetch him a drink of water, please,' Dad said.

I looked at Mum.

'Oh, all right,' she agreed, 'get it a drink, but only in something we can throw away after.'

I came back with some water in an old plastic box and put it on the step. Rocky unwrapped himself from Dad's legs and took a few sips, then drank the lot without stopping for breath.

'I think he must be hungry as well,' said Darren, 'he's all skin and bones.'

'I keep telling you the dog's an athlete,' said Dad. 'This is his running weight.'

'Parched and starved is more like it,' argued Mum. 'Bring it something to eat, Darren. There's a meat pie in the fridge.'

'You can't give a greyhound meat pie ...' Dad started to protest, but Darren was already back from the kitchen with Dad's dinner. Rocky's ears pricked up for the first time the moment he smelt food and in no time he'd finished the lot.

'Did you see that?' said Darren, as Rocky licked the plate clean. 'He never even chewed it, just sucked it up like a Hoover!'

'All right, all right, just this once,' Dad gave in, 'but in future he has to have a proper balanced diet.'

'What do you mean, *in future*?' Mum was even more furious. 'That animal has got no future here! First thing tomorrow morning, you take it back where it came from and get our money back! Until then, it stays outside where I can't see it.'

Dad opened his mouth to argue, but Mum had already stormed off. That left the three of us – and the dog.

'Well,' Dad said at last, 'I expect she'll come round.'

You'd think he'd know by now that Mum *never* comes round once she's made her mind up about something.

'Anyway,' Dad went on, 'I'm famished. What's for me dinner?'

Darren and I looked at each other, then we both looked at Rocky, who was quietly wiping his mouth round the back of Dad's jeans.

CHAPTER 2

I thought Dad took it pretty well when we told him Rocky had eaten his meat pie. He seemed happy to make do with the jam sandwich and Mars bar I got for him. Rocky clung tightly to Dad's legs, watching him eat every mouthful.

Then we stood about, wondering what to do next.

'Shall we take him for a walk?' suggested Darren.

'Good thinking, son!' Dad was all enthusiastic again. 'Greyhounds need plenty of exercise. A few times round the park's just the thing! Are you coming, Anna?'

I wasn't sure what to do. Part of me said I ought to go and find Mum and try to cheer her up. But when Mum's in one of her bad moods she can get angry with anybody and I didn't want her shouting at me.

'All right,' I agreed, 'if I can walk with Rocky.'

I'd always wanted a dog of my own to take for a walk. And it looked like this was the only chance I was going to get, what with Mum saying we couldn't keep him.

Rocky didn't even have a proper collar and lead – just an old bit of rope tied round his neck. I gave it a tug. Nothing happened. So I tugged it harder. Still nothing.

Dad bent down and started making those silly clucking noises that people make when they talk to babies and animals, and slapping his legs. 'Come on, boy! Come on, Rocky!' he kept calling.

But Rocky didn't budge. It was like his paws were glued to the path.

'Let me try,' said Darren.

He took some old jelly babies out of his pocket and put one in the palm of his hand. Then he held it in front of Rocky's nose, so he would have to walk forward if he wanted to eat it.

It worked! Darren had actually had a good idea (although I didn't say so). One leg at a time, Rocky started to creep forward, until he reached Darren's hand and snaffled up his reward.

'Come on, Rocky! Walkies!' called Darren, only this time he held the next sweet further away

Four jelly babies later and we were out of the gate and on the road to the park. Now Rocky had got going, we didn't dare stop.

'But Dad,' I said, 'I don't think Rocky should be eating all these sweets. What about his special diet?'

'Don't worry about that, Anna. Sugar's a high-energy food. He'll burn it all off as soon as he gets to an open space.' Dad actually sounded like he knew what he was talking about.

'And shouldn't he be marking his territory or whatever you call it?' I asked.

'You mean weeing all over the place,' suggested Darren.

You see, I couldn't help noticing that Rocky didn't do any of the things that normal dogs usually do, like sniffing or cocking his leg, or even growling a bit. He just kept plodding forward, with his head down and his tail between his legs.

'Rocky's saving his energy,' Dad had an answer for everything. 'Wait till we let him off the lead, then he'll go like lightening.'

We'd just reached the park, when Darren ran out of sweets. Without any more rewards, Rocky gave up moving. His legs collapsed and he lay down in a large, shaky heap.

'Come on, Rocky! Let's go! Come on boy!' Darren ran around, waving his arms and shouting. Then he threw a stick. 'Fetch, Rocky! Go, Rocky!' he kept calling.

Rocky shut his eyes.

That was when three of the rough boys from Darren's class came riding up on their bikes.

'Whotcha got there, Darren?' called Marcus

Harding, the biggest and nastiest.

Darren went bright red. It's no use Mum telling him that Marcus and his friends have got behavioural difficulties and to ignore them. I know Darren thinks they're really cool.

'That another stupid present off yer dad?' Marcus sniggered, so the others copied him.

'Look's like Darren's taking his dog for a nice lie down!' one of them sneered.

'Clear off, you lot! I know where you live!' shouted Dad, which only made Darren even more embarrassed.

The three boys had a good laugh at that, but I knew they wouldn't try anything on while Dad was there. They made do with riding round us a few times and shouting swear words from a safe distance.

Darren was mortified. 'What did you have to bring that stupid dog home for?' he yelled.

'Now come on, son, Rocky's just a bit tired. I expect he's had a big race and he needs some time to get over it,' Dad started.

'He can't even walk, so how can he run? He's useless, like everything else you do! I'm glad Mum's making you take him back!' Darren was really angry, although I could see how hard he was trying not to cry.

Dad went to put his arm round him, but Darren turned and ran away. Dad tried calling after him, but it was no use. Nothing ever worked when Darren got into a strop.

'Don't worry about him. He's always running off. He'll go straight back home,' I told Dad.

There's not a lot you can do in the park with a sleeping dog, so we decided to go home as well. Dad managed to get Rocky on his feet again, but nothing would make him move. He looked absolutely terrified by the open space all around him. His eyes were wide and staring and he was shaking all over.

In the end, Dad picked Rocky up and carried him. We got a lot a strange looks from people and I hung behind as much as I could, pretending I wasn't with them.

Surely even Dad could see a dog you had to carry home was never going to win any races? No wonder Mum was furious. Dad's always having these daft ideas for making money, but this time he'd really messed things up. Even getting that broken-down burger van, which sat on the front lawn for a year, seemed clever compared with buying an old greyhound.

Dad put Rocky down when we got inside our gate, just in time for him to do the most enormous wee all over the path.

'Yucko!' I said, jumping out of the way. Thank goodness Mum hadn't seen it.

'Look at that, Anna!' Even Rocky going to the toilet made Dad all excited. 'Now he's marking his territory! That means he thinks he belongs here!'

'But he's not staying. Mum says you have to take him back in the morning,' I reminded him.

'This dog's a fortune on four legs, Anna. All we have to do is get your Mum to see it.'

Was Dad really talking about the same dog? Since when had anyone been able to convince Mum she was wrong? And what was all this about how *'we'* had to do it?

CHAPTER 3

We walked round to the back door. Then Dad hesitated. 'You go on in, Anna,' he said. 'I'll just take Rocky down the shed – he's not used to the indoor life.'

At least Dad had enough sense to keep out of Mum's way. I watched both of them walk off down the garden. I felt really sorry for Rocky as he crept along – he seemed such a poor, sad thing, which was when it hit me. Nobody was thinking about Rocky at all. Dad didn't even notice how thin and neglected he looked; Mum didn't care – she just wanted her money back, and all Darren worried about was what stupid Marcus Harding said.

Rocky must have come from a really bad home to end up like this, and now we were planning to send him back. How cruel was that? And I was the only one getting upset about it! There had to be a way out and I realised it was down to me to try and find it.

The minute I went in the house, I could tell I didn't stand much chance. There was this horrible atmosphere, like the air was full of electricity and only needed a spark to make it explode. The PlayStation was blasting away upstairs, so I guessed Darren was back in his bedroom. Mum was in the kitchen, ironing furiously. I could see she'd been crying, because her eyes were all red. I knew how upset she was by how loudly she was banging the iron down and the amount of steam coming off the clothes.

'And before you ask me, Anna, the answer's no,' Mum jumped in before I'd even said anything.

'But Mum ...'

'I know what you're going to say and the answer's no; that dog's not staying here.'

'But I hadn't asked ...'

'No, but you were going to.'

Mum was right. I did want us to keep Rocky – not to race him or anything but because he needed looking after.

'And don't look at me like that!' Mum snapped.

'Like what?' Wrong answer.

'Like I'm some sort of animal hater or dog killer!' Mum was shouting now.

I felt my eyes start to fill up. It wasn't fair that she was taking it all out on me.

Mum put the iron down, came over and gave me a hug. 'I'm sorry, love,' she said, a lot more calmly.

15

'I'm angry with your Dad, not you. What he's done is doubly cruel this time – it was wrong to bring that poor dog here and it's worse to make you and Darren so upset.'

'But it's not Rocky's fault!' I began.

'No, it's your Dad's fault and this time he's going to put it right.'

'If it's the money, I could save up …' I tried.

'That money belonged to all of us, Anna,' Mum went on. 'We don't have 50p to spare, let alone a hundred pounds. Have you got any idea how many shelves I have to fill at Tesco's or how many hours I have to work for that sort of money?'

'Loads, I suppose,' I mumbled.

'Right. But your Dad didn't stop to think about that – he never does. He's too busy throwing away the money I've had to work for on one ridiculous plan after another. But this is the last time, believe me Anna, this is going to be the very last time. I mean it.'

Then Mum gave me her look: the one that says she'd had the final word and don't you dare say anything else or there'll be big trouble. So I just gave in. I was letting Rocky down, but I didn't want Mum to start shouting at me again.

The rest of the evening was awful. Dad stayed out of sight. Later on I heard the gate slam, so I suppose he'd got fed up dog-sitting and gone off somewhere.

Darren wouldn't come out of his room, even at teatime, so that left Mum and me on our own. Mum tried to be chatty and kept asking me stuff about school, but it didn't cover up how bad we were both feeling.

When Mum went off to watch television, I crept out to see how Rocky was doing. The shed's not a bad place to leave a dog in. It's Dad's 'private space', and he's fixed it up really well, with shelves and a piece of carpet and an old armchair. Dad calls it his workshop, though Mum says it's a rubbish dump where he goes to hide when she wants any jobs doing.

Rocky seemed cosy enough. Dad had put an old blanket on the floor for him to lie on. There was a saucepan of fresh water and a bowl for food that he'd licked to a shine. I gave him some biscuits. I didn't care about his racing diet: Rocky looked like a dog who needed a few treats. I stroked his head and rubbed behind his ears, and eventually he stopped shaking and even lay down next to me. He felt lovely and warm, like a furry hot water bottle.

'Sorry, Rocky,' I whispered, 'I did try but we can't keep you.'

I felt in such a muddle about everything. Mum's always falling out with Dad over stuff, but this time it was loads worse. I needed Dad to get our money back, because Mum had said it was his last chance. I was really scared about what might happen to us, if Dad didn't take Rocky back. But I couldn't stop worrying about what would become of Rocky if he did.

'Goodnight Rocky,' I said, as I got up to go. Then I closed the shed door before I could see him look at me with those big, sad eyes.

CHAPTER 4

It was late when I heard Dad come in, but I hadn't been to sleep at all. I kept tossing and turning, trying to think of a way Dad could possibly get out of trouble, but without hurting Rocky. No matter how hard I tried, I couldn't come up with one good idea.

I guessed Mum had been lying awake as well, because she started shouting as soon as Dad opened their bedroom door. I put the pillow over my head to try and shut out the noise, but some of the words still got through:

'… get a proper job … sick and tired … bills to pay and food to buy … how could you?' Mum was yelling.

'Wait a minute, Jo,' I heard Dad begin and I held my breath, hoping he'd say something that would make it all right.

But Mum didn't even stop to listen; she just went on and on, until: '… and that's your final warning!'

she shouted.

Then I heard their door slam, followed by Dad's footsteps going downstairs. I expect he was going to sleep on the settee.

I was used to Mum and Dad rowing, but I'd never heard them this bad before. My heart was pounding and I felt all shaky, like when you've run a bit too fast and you have to sit down – except I was already in bed. I thought of calling out for Mum, but I didn't want her to know I'd been listening. Besides, I was scared of seeing how upset she might be.

I must have finally dropped off to sleep, when some terrible noise suddenly jolted me wide awake. At first, I thought it was the alarm clock, but when I looked it was only two o'clock in the morning. I must have dreamt it.

I shut my eyes, when there it was again: an ear-piercing yowl, like something in the most terrible pain. It stopped for a moment, then carried on even louder, as if someone had turned the volume control up full. And this time it went on and on.

'Anna, are you all right? Whatever's the matter?' Mum came bursting in.

Darren was right behind her, rubbing his eyes and with his hair all sticking up. 'Enemy attack, take cover; repeat, take cover,' he mumbled.

'It's not me, Mum,' I told her, getting out of bed, 'I think it's coming from outside.'

My bedroom's at the back of the house, so we opened the curtains and looked down the garden. There was no mistaking where the noise was coming from: the shed.

'It's that wretched dog!' exclaimed Mum.

We all just stood there as if we couldn't believe our ears, while Rocky's howling rose to new, head-splitting heights.

'Wow!' said Darren, 'Rocky can do that?'

'Then it's a pity his legs aren't as good as his lungs,' Mum snapped back.

All at once, the whole place was lit up in a blaze of light as next-door's security beams came on.

'Oh no! Don't say that animal's woken Old Wilf!' cried Mum.

Old Wilf's our ancient next-door neighbour. Mum calls him 'That Old Fossil', because he's always complaining about us, and he calls us 'You Horrible Lot'.

We saw Wilf come tottering out his back door, wearing an old coat over a pair of striped pyjamas. He headed down the path towards our shed. Then he climbed onto the garden chair he keeps for looking over our fence and started banging on the shed roof with his walking stick.

'Shut up! Shut up!!' shouted Wilf each time the stick came down.

'Quick, Mum!' I grabbed her arm, 'you've got to

do something – he's frightening Rocky!'

'SHUT UP!!! SHUT UP!!!' The louder Wilf shouted, the louder Rocky howled.

Now we weren't the only people awake. All around us lights were being turned on and curtains pulled, while anxious faces stared out from upstairs windows.

'Rocky's waking the whole street!' said Darren proudly.

'That's all we need!' Mum cried. 'We'll have the police here next! Where on earth's your Dad?'

The three of us raced downstairs and into the living room. Gentle snoring noises were coming from the settee. Dad had to be the only person for miles who was still asleep. Mum grabbed one end of the sleeping bag and pulled Dad off onto the floor.

'Wassa matter ...? Wos up ...?' he mumbled.

'The whole street's up!' shouted Mum. 'That animal is howling its head off and Old Wilf's breaking the shed down – that's what's the matter. Get out there and sort it out!'

'Hurry up, please Dad,' I said, throwing him his jeans, 'before Rocky gets hurt!'

'All right, all right, love,' said Dad as he struggled into his clothes.

'And don't come back in this house till that dog's quiet!' Mum stamped out.

'Rocky's in trouble now, isn't he Dad?' asked

Darren.

'Go on, you two, get back to bed,' Dad told us.

'But he will be all right though, won't he?' I asked.

'Course he will, love,' Dad tried to reassure me, 'he's just a bit frightened being in a strange place. Don't worry, I'll make sure he's OK.'

Darren went back to his room, but I didn't go straight to bed. I went over to the window and watched Dad go down the garden and open the shed door. Immediately, Rocky stopped howling. Then I heard Dad trying to calm Old Wilf down. Wilf did a lot of swearing and shouting, but eventually he climbed off the chair and hobbled back inside.

Dad turned to my window and gave me a big thumbs-up, to show me Rocky was all right. Then darkness descended again as the security lights blinked off. Gradually the lights in all the other houses went out too.

I got back under the duvet and let the silence fold in around me. Things were bad before, but I couldn't believe how much trouble Dad was in now. Still, I was too exhausted to lie awake worrying anymore.

It was nearly ten o'clock in the morning when I finally woke up. Thank goodness it was a Sunday so I'd been able to sleep in. I was the only person about; Mum had already gone to work, Darren was still in bed and Dad was nowhere to be seen.

I filled a bowl with fresh water and went down the shed to see how Rocky was doing. I couldn't believe my eyes when I opened the door. There was Dad snoring in the armchair. On his lap, and wrapped in the same blanket, was Rocky; also fast asleep, with his head resting peacefully on Dad's shoulder.

CHAPTER 5

I was finishing my breakfast when Dad came into the kitchen.

'Morning, Anna!' he said brightly and gave me a big hug. He didn't seem a bit like someone who'd spent the night in a shed.

Dad made himself a cup of tea and began searching through the cupboards until he found a tin of corned beef. 'I'll just give this to Rocky and then I'll be off,' he told me.

'That's not proper food for …' I started to say, but didn't finish. Rocky wasn't going to be our dog for much longer, so there was no point making a fuss.

I got up to go and say goodbye to Rocky, and then sat back down. It was better to stay away, as I'd only get upset again as soon as I saw him. I made myself a promise. From now on I'd only think about things getting better at home, and not about abandoning Rocky.

Dad was back. 'You couldn't lend me a few quid, could you, Anna?'

'What for?' I asked suspiciously.

'Oh – I just need to get a few bits and pieces for Rocky,' he explained vaguely. 'Go on, please Anna; I'll pay you back.'

When Dad said it was for Rocky, I didn't stop to think. I went upstairs to fetch the old sweet tin I use as a moneybox and emptied it out onto the table.

'Thanks, sweetheart,' Dad scooped up every penny and put it in his pocket. There was nearly twenty pounds, because I'd been saving for ages to buy a pair of those new skinny jeans. 'But don't tell Mum, will you, love?' he added, closing the door quickly behind him.

I heard Dad go whistling down our drive. He seemed very cheerful this morning. He hadn't made any fuss over taking Rocky back. And he'd got all my money, and he didn't want Mum to know.

Then I began to get that sick feeling in my stomach, like when you carry on eating the last piece of chocolate, even though you're already full up. Dad was planning something – and I must have been half-asleep not to notice it before. I had to find a way to stop him, but there wasn't much time.

I couldn't leave Darren by himself, so I ran up to his bedroom and pulled the covers off him.

'Go 'way,' he grumbled.

'Get up, quick, Darren!' I shouted. 'Dad's supposed to be taking Rocky back, but I'm sure he's doing something else. We've got to find out what he's up to.'

That woke Darren up. 'Wicked!' he said, jumping out of bed and throwing his clothes on over his pyjamas.

I could hear Dad trying to start our old car. I was counting on it taking ages, like it always did, but he could drive off at any moment. Darren ran down the stairs after me and we both raced out the house.

We were in luck! Dad was still turning the engine over when we flung the passenger doors open. Rocky was stretched out along the back seat, taking up most of the room with his long legs. Darren pushed him over and squashed himself in the bit of space that was left, while I got in the front.

'Hey! What on earth's going on?' Dad said in surprise.

'We're going with you,' I said, putting on my seatbelt.

'OUT, both of you! NOW!' Dad exclaimed.

'No way!' I told him. 'Either you take us with you, or I'm ringing Mum now – about this!' I shook my empty moneybox at him.

'And I'll tell her we were frightened to be at home on our own,' continued Darren, 'and you wouldn't let us go with you, even though I cried and cried, and ...'

'All right!' Dad gave in. 'But you both keep quiet and do everything I tell you, OK?'

I nodded, but crossed my fingers – just in case.

The engine started at last and we set off. Rocky perked up straight away. He sat up with his nose resting against the window, looking out on the world like some celebrity being chauffeur-driven to his next important engagement.

'Where are we going,' I asked, 'is it far?'

'Shouldn't take us long, love,' Dad replied.

'And what did you really borrow my money for?' I persisted.

'Mum says never lend Dad any money or that's the last you'll see of it,' put in Darren smugly.

'I've just got to sort something out before …' Dad's answers were getting more and more vague.

'But you're only supposed to drop Rocky off and get our hundred pounds,' I went on. 'Aren't you?'

'Yeah, like Mum told you,' Darren added.

Dad didn't reply. Now we were driving through part of town I'd never seen before. I could feel that horrible sick feeling come back, but even stronger this time.

'Dad – what's going on?' I asked again. 'Please, you've got to tell us!'

At that moment, I saw where we were heading. The place had a sign with a picture of two racing dogs in full flight and the words *Greyhound Stadium*. It was the dog track. On the back seat, Rocky pricked up his ears and let out a low whine, as if he knew where he was.

'Now listen you two – I've got this great plan!' said Dad at last. I couldn't bear to hear how enthusiastic he sounded.

'You're not going to take Rocky back, are you?' I whispered. 'You never meant to take him back all along.'

'Wait till Mum finds out about this!' said Darren happily. 'She'll kill you. Dad, you are so dead already!'

CHAPTER 6

Dad took a left turn opposite the main entrance and pulled up in a pub car park. The pub was called *The Dog and Rabbit*, and had a sign showing a smiling greyhound bearing down on a small, terrified animal. It was hard to imagine Rocky frightening anything. It seemed far more likely that he'd be the one running away.

'Wait here with Rocky, both of you,' said Dad, turning off the engine, 'and I'll be back soon.'

'No way!' I was really mad with him. 'You tell us what's going on, or Darren and I are getting out of this car and walking home!' I grabbed the handle and started opening the car door to show I meant it.

'That's right, Dad,' said Darren, 'even though we don't know the way back. Then Mum'll kill you twice over.'

'All right, all right,' Dad sighed. 'If you really have to know, it's like this. My mate Gary has got a cousin whose friend knows this bloke called Des.'

'I'm lost already,' said Darren.

'Shut up Darren,' I told him. 'Go on, Dad.'

'Now Des drinks here, at this pub. And he knows people at the dog track. So Gary says if I slip him a few quid ...'

'That's why Dad wanted your money, Anna!' interrupted Darren again.

'... he'll put in a word and get Rocky into a big race – one where the real money is.'

'But you promised Mum you were taking Rocky back and now you're trying to race him!' This was even worse than I thought. 'What are you going to do when she finds out? What about the hundred pounds you owe her?'

'And what about getting Rocky to run? He hasn't even walked yet,' added Darren.

On the back seat Rocky had gone to sleep, oblivious to all the noise we were making.

'Look,' said Dad, 'I didn't actually make Mum a promise did I? I didn't actually *say* I was taking Rocky back, so I haven't told Mum any lies have I? Besides, Rocky's a winner – I know he is. He just needs the atmosphere, the excitement of the track. Now here's the clever bit!'

Clever? Dad thought he was being clever?

'This is what we do. We get Rocky in a big race, put our money on him ...'

'But we haven't got any money,' I tried to point out, while Dad ignored me.

'… and when he wins, that hundred quid becomes five hundred – perhaps even a thousand pounds! And that's just the start!'

I'd had enough. 'This is the stupidest thing I've ever heard of! Come on Dad; let's just take Rocky back, like we're supposed to. Darren and I won't say anything to Mum, will we Darren?'

'We might …' Darren began.

'No we won't!' I shot Darren a dirty look. 'Come on Dad, it's not too late.'

It was like I hadn't spoken.

'This is going to work, Anna,' Dad persisted. 'I know Rocky can change things for this family. I just need you to give us both a chance – please.'

There was nothing left for me to say. I could see Dad's mind was made up and once he gets an idea in his head there's no arguing with him. I was too choked up to speak, so I just nodded my head.

'Good girl, Anna,' said Dad happily. 'I can't wait to see your Mum's face when she hears the news!'

That's exactly why I was so upset, but Dad didn't notice. He'd already got out of the car and vanished into the pub.

Darren had that frowny look he gets when he's thinking. 'Dad might have a good idea this time, don't you think so, Anna?' he asked eventually.

'No.'

'Rocky might get in a big race …'

'No.'

'And he might win …'

'No.'

'Then we'll have lots of money …'

'No.'

'And I can have an iPod and a new computer.'

'NO,' I shouted, 'don't be so stupid! None of those things will happen, ever, so shut up about it, will you?'

'I just thought perhaps this once …'

'Then start thinking properly! Remember the time Dad bought two hundred tins of baked beans to find the lucky prize label, which he never did, and we had to eat beans every day for six months?'

Darren nodded.

'And when he started window cleaning, and got stuck up the ladder because he can't stand heights?'

'Yeah, I remember.'

'Or when he started delivering *Pete's Organic Home-Grown Produce*, until someone found out he'd just bought all the vegetables from the supermarket and rubbed dirt on them? So Mum had to give all the customers back twice what they'd paid before anyone called the police? And she was so mad, Dad had to go and stay at Gran's for two weeks?'

'All right, I get the point,' sulked Darren.

'Well, this is a million times worse,' I went on, 'and if Mum sends Dad to Gran's this time, I don't think he'll ever come home again!'

The words had tumbled out my mouth before I could stop them. It was the one thing I'd been dreading all along and now I'd said it. And saying it only made it more real.

I tried to say sorry to Darren, but he had his face buried in Rocky's side. Rocky was still asleep and making low, snuffling noises. Perhaps he was chasing that rabbit in his dreams.

CHAPTER 7

We never noticed Dad come back, so we both jumped when he banged on the window.

'Hurry up! Get Rocky out! Des is coming!' Dad said excitedly.

Darren pushed and I pulled and between us we manoeuvred Rocky out of the car. He made straight for Dad and wrapped himself around his knees. Then the four of us stood in line like we were waiting for a bus.

'He wants to see Rocky for himself. Now leave all the talking to me,' said Dad.

A scruffy bloke with a grey, straggly ponytail and a gold hoop in one ear walked across the car park. He came straight up to Rocky and began stroking him.

'Well, if it isn't Sheldon Rocket,' said Des, the man who was going to help make our fortune. 'Never thought I'd see you again, my son.'

'I told you it was him,' said Dad proudly.

'But how do you know? It could be any old dog!' Darren butted in. I expect he was being stroppy because I'd upset him.

'Darren, go and wait in the car!' Dad ordered, but Darren didn't move.

'The lad's got a fair question,' said Des. 'Anyone who goes down the dogs would recognise Sheldon a mile away. Never seen another greyhound with those markings – you could always pick out that eye patch and his one odd leg. Besides, he won three times in a row at Portsmouth last year, and I never forget a winner, especially when I've put my own money on him.'

'There, I told you all along Rocky was a winner! Do you believe me now, Anna?' put in Dad.

I was too furious with Dad for planning all this to answer. Besides, it all sounded too good to be true.

'Then you've only got to look in his ear,' Des carried on.

'What for? He's not deaf!' Darren was really pushing it now.

'Don't be smart, sonny,' Des said. 'Don't you know nothing about racing dogs? They all have to be licensed to run, then they gets a special number tattooed in their ears.'

Des gently lifted up Rocky's ear, and we all leaned over to have a look. Sure enough, we could read NTS1, clearly marked in blue ink.

'And that same number'll be on the paperwork your Dad's got – tells him he's bought the right dog,' Des explained.

Dad took a tatty bit of paper out of his pocket and showed it to us. 'Here's Rocky's number, just like Des said. Proves we own a champion!'

'But just look at the state of him,' Des stroked Rocky some more. 'How'd you get in this mess, old chap?'

'No need to worry about that,' said Dad, 'we'll soon get him back to top form. Now I wanted to talk to you about ...'

'Often wondered what happened to Mr Sheldon Rocket,' Des carried on, 'after his old owner died and all his dogs were sold off. Always hoped he'd get a good home. But there's not many folks that'll take on a greyhound what can't race any more.'

'C-c-can't race?' Dad spluttered. 'What do you mean – *can't race*?'

I knew it! I knew there had to be something wrong.

Des looked amazed. 'You're telling me you don't know what happened?'

Dad shook his head.

'I was there on the night,' Des began, 'the Rocket's last race. The starter went and he shot out that trap like a real rocket. He was all set to win by a mile, only he came too fast round the last bend – ran smack into

37

the barrier. Broke his leg. He'll never run again.'

Dad's face had turned pale. At last he must have realised what a terrible mess he was in.

'You didn't buy the dog to race him, did you?' Des asked, as if he couldn't believe it.

Dad's mouth hung open, but he couldn't get a word out. He just nodded.

'Well, all I can say is that somebody has taken you for a proper ride.'

'That's just what our Mum says ... Ow! Anna, that hurt!' Darren shut up when I jabbed him in the ribs.

We all turned to Rocky. Sure enough, once you looked closely, you could see that he was holding one of his back legs slightly off the ground. Poor dog!

'Where'd you find him?' asked Des. 'Person treats a dog like that should be shot.'

Yes, I thought, and I wanted to be the one who did it.

'This fella came in the pub yesterday,' Dad spoke at last, very quietly. 'Short bloke, black curly hair. Said his name was Mick.'

'Pierced lip and eyebrow?' Des asked and Dad nodded.

'Sounds like Big Mick. Always hanging round the track, trying his luck. Do anything for a few quid. I dunno how he got his hands on old Sheldon. Wouldn't trust him with a rat, let alone a dog.'

'You don't happen to know where this Big Mick

lives, do you Des?' Dad's face had turned from white to red. He looked like he'd explode any minute.

'Sure, everyone knows where to find Big Mick. Not the sort of bloke you'd want to visit though,' Des replied.

I heard him give Dad some long, complicated directions, then they shook hands. 'Get yourself a drink on me, mate,' Dad told him, pulling a handful of change (my money!) out of his pocket.

'No, no, keep your money,' Des pushed Dad's hand away. 'Buy Mr Rocket here something – he's brought me good luck in the past, now it looks like he needs some himself.' Then he turned round and walked off back to the pub.

As soon as Des was out of sight, Dad threw the car doors open and bundled Rocky into the back.

'Come on you lot,' he told us, 'get in quick. We're going to sort this out.'

CHAPTER 8

'Slow down, Dad!' I yelled, as he swung the car round and we raced off with the tyres screeching.

'Rocky hasn't even got his seat belt on yet,' joked Darren. He'd forgotten about being miserable – this was much too exciting.

Dad put his foot on the brake until we reached a safe speed, but he couldn't keep calm any longer. 'That dirty, stinking, lying, cheating, evil, miserable, TOE RAG!' he shouted.

'Why don't you say what you really think, Dad?' Darren teased.

'And I don't want to hear any more of your smart-alecky remarks for the rest of the day, do you understand?' Dad jumped at him.

Dad never loses his temper with us, never, so now we knew how really angry he was. Darren shut up and pretended to be very interested in looking out the window. I wanted to say, 'I told you so, Dad, ' as it was all his own stupid fault in the first place, but I kept quiet as well.

We drove out of town and into the countryside in total silence.

'But Dad, where are we going? What are you going to do?' I asked eventually.

'Do?' Dad repeated. 'Do? What do you think I'm going to do? I'm going to take that useless three-and-a-half legged lump back to the thieving individual who sold him to me and get our money back!'

Rocky's ears pricked up as if he knew we were talking about him, then he flopped back down with his head on Darren's lap.

'Des seemed to think he might not like visitors ...' I began.

But there was no stopping Dad now. 'Then we'll give him a big surprise, won't we?' he shouted.

I waited for Darren to say it might be us getting the surprise, but even he had the sense not to.

'And we haven't got much time left before your Mum gets home,' Dad remembered.

That brought me down to earth with a jolt – I hadn't thought about Mum for ages. Whatever was she going to say when she found out what Dad had been up to? But there might still be time to sort everything out. If I could somehow persuade Darren to keep quiet about today, and if Dad got the money, she might forgive

41

him. And I wouldn't think about poor Rocky and his broken leg, I wouldn't: just like I'd promised myself this morning.

After another ten minutes we came to a big roundabout, where we turned off onto a narrow side road surrounded by empty fields. Dad started driving really slowly, peering through the windscreen like he was looking for something.

'Gotcha!' he said suddenly.

He swung sharp right through an opening in a hedge and onto a dirt track. We bounced and shook along over the potholes. Rocky started to whine and turn round and round on the seat. Only there wasn't enough room, so he was walking all over Darren and smacking him in the face with his tail.

The track curved round and came to an end. Dad stopped the car and switched off the engine: everywhere was silent, apart from a few birds calling. It felt like we were miles from nowhere.

The place gave me the shivers, 'Who'd want to live here?' I said.

In front of us was this tumbledown shack. It was built out of an old caravan, with other bits and pieces stuck on around it. There was a lean-to with a tin roof on one side, part of a wooden shed stuck on the other and a porch made from old doors and windows at the front.

'Dad,' whispered Darren, 'I don't like it.'

I thought perhaps he'd gone back to messing about, but he wasn't making it up – he really did look frightened. And that made two of us: three if you counted Rocky. He was whining loudly now, and scrabbling around on the back seat.

'Quick, Dad,' I begged, 'let's turn round and go home, before somebody comes.'

'Well, that's pretty good, coming from the person who wanted me to take the dog back not long ago!' Dad snapped. 'You two wait here, while I go and find this Big Mick.'

'No, Dad! Don't leave us!' Darren sounded like he could burst into tears any minute.

'Darren's right; there's no way we're stopping on our own in this place,' I said.

Dad could see we were both scared and he stopped being cross with us. 'Look, you know I've got to do this,' he said in a much kinder voice, 'so come on, but stick close to me.'

We had to almost drag Rocky out of the car. His ears went up and he started pulling on his rope lead so hard that Dad had trouble holding him. It was horrible seeing Rocky like this. I was sure he recognised the place – and was desperate to get away.

Dad led us all up to the door and banged loudly. 'Hello! Hello!' he shouted, but there was no reply.

Everywhere I looked was piled high with junk. There were heaps of plastic containers, newspapers and other rubbish on the ground or caught up in the nearby branches, and all sorts of rusty bits of metal. A car with no wheels and doors was so overgrown with ivy it had nearly vanished into the woods.

'Come on, Dad, there's nobody here, let's go,' I said. I didn't want us to find anybody. And I didn't care about the money any more: all I wanted was for us to leave as fast as we could.

Then we spotted an ancient van with the bonnet up. There were two legs sticking out from underneath. Dad strode over, with me and Darren struggling to keep up with him.

'Hello! Hello!' Dad shouted again, banging his fist on the roof of the wreck.

There was a big thump, lots of muffled swearing and then the person at the end of the legs crawled out, rubbing his head where he must have hit it. He had headphones on, which was why he hadn't heard us.

'What are you doing here? You scared the life out of me!' he said. Actually, that's what he said with all the swear words missed out.

There was no mistaking Big Mick after Des's description of him. Although he only came up to Dad's shoulder, he was twice as wide. He smelt like a mixture of stale beer, cigarette smoke and old socks. I didn't like the way he was holding on to a huge spanner, or how he was looking at us.

Darren crept up to Dad and took hold of his hand.

44

Rocky was trying to squirm between the two of them. He was trembling all over and his back leg, the one he'd broken, was shaking uncontrollably.

I looked around helplessly, trying to work out how quickly we could all run back to our car, but it was already too late.

CHAPTER 9

Dad stepped forward, putting Darren, Rocky and me behind him. 'Remember me?' he asked, bending over to look Big Mick right in the eyes.

'Naw, never seen yer before,' the man snarled back. He spat on the ground, just missing Dad's foot.

'Then you remember him, don't you?' Dad pointed at Rocky.

'That old dog? What's it to me?'

'It's a hundred quid of my money for a so-called champion greyhound that turned out to be a useless mutt, that's what it is!' Dad was losing his temper again and I held my breath.

'Don't know what you're talking about. Go on, clear off, the lot of yer!' Big Mick was shouting now, and waving the spanner about. 'This here's private property and you're trespassing!'

I was already scared: now I was terrified. We were miles away from any help and Dad didn't seem to realise what he was getting into.

Darren tugged on Dad's sleeve. 'I want to go home,' he whispered.

'Yeah, get on out of it before I calls the cops!' Big Mick snarled.

This was our chance to leave, but Dad wouldn't back down. Perhaps the thought of going back to Mum empty-handed seemed even worse than what Big Mick might do.

'Now that's a good idea,' Dad said, all cool and calm, 'let's give the police a ring and the RSPCA and …'

'You're off your head, that's what you are, mate,' Mick sniggered.

Dad took out his mobile. 'They'll soon sort it out. And while they're here they might want to have a good look round. Then who knows what else they might find?'

He started to punch in the numbers.

You could almost see the wheels turning in Big Mick's head as he tried to work out what to do. Finally, he took a step back and put the spanner down. 'Hang on a minute, now hang on. Perhaps I do know yer after all.'

Dad hesitated for a moment, then put the phone away. I gasped for air, realising I'd been holding my breath all this time. It looked like Dad might be able to talk our way out of here, after all.

'You know me all right,' Dad told Big Mick. 'I paid you a hundred quid for this dog yesterday – the one you told me was a champion racer.'

'That's Sheldon Rocket!' exclaimed Big Mick indignantly, forgetting he didn't recognise Rocky. 'He's won more races than I've had hot dinners!'

'Until he broke his leg, so he can't run any more. Only you didn't tell me that, did you?' Dad continued.

'What yer talking about? I sold you that greyhound in good faith. Don't know nothing about no broken leg.'

'That's not what I've heard. So, here's the dog back. Now give me the money you owe me and we're out of here,' Dad persisted.

'Now you really are out of yer mind!' Big Mick spluttered.

'Or perhaps I'd better call the cops after all and see what they make of all this.'

'All right! All right!' Big Mick reached into his pocket and pulled out three crumpled ten-pound notes. 'Here, take it and get lost!'

Dad looked at the money in amazement. 'And the rest of it! A hundred quid you had off me, A HUNDRED!'

But Dad had pushed things too far.

'Who d'yer think you are, coming here and calling me a liar?' yelled Big Mick, poking Dad in the shoulder with a grubby finger. 'Thirty quid's what yer getting – take it or leave it!'

We all edged back. My heart was beating so fast I thought it would burst through my chest. 'Please Dad,' I thought, 'get us out of here.'

Dad turned to me. 'If I take this money and borrow your twenty pounds, Anna, I'll have half the money to give your Mum,' he said quietly. 'It's better than nothing.'

'But look at Rocky, Dad,' Darren said, 'he's terrified! We can't leave him!'

Darren was right; I could hardly bear to look at the poor dog.

Dad made a decision. He walked over to Big Mick. 'Done,' he told him, and snatched the notes the man was holding out. 'Come on, boy.'

Dad pulled Rocky forward. Rocky gave a piercing yelp and began to pull in the opposite direction.

'Don't Dad!' I called out. 'You mustn't!' I didn't care about what Mum thought, or the money now – saving Rocky mattered much more.

'Give him 'ere!' snapped Big Mick, and snatched Rocky's lead. Rocky lost his footing and skidded across the ground. 'Get up, you useless mongrel!' Big Mick shouted, and hit him with the end of the rope.

Rocky began to whimper and tried to cringe away. 'Shut yer noise!' yelled Big Mick and aimed a kick at Rocky's side.

'Don't you hurt Rocky!' Darren darted forward, but Dad managed to grab hold of him.

'Do something, Dad!' I shouted.

'There's nothing I can do,' Dad snapped back, 'Rocky's not ours any more.'

Rocky looked up when he heard Dad's voice and tried to reach him, but Big Mick was holding his lead too tightly. 'Shut up, you stupid mutt!' he yelled and jerked on the rope till Rocky started choking.

Then, all of a sudden, something seemed to come over Dad.

'Hey!' he called out. 'No need to treat the dog like that.'

'What's it to you? You've got yer money. Dog's mine and I'll treat him how I likes,' Big Mick snarled.

I watched open-mouthed as Dad grabbed Rocky's lead out of Big Mick's hand and stuffed the money in his jacket pocket.

'Deal's off,' Dad told him, 'I've changed my mind. Keep your money and leave my dog alone!' He turned to us, 'Darren, Anna, get in the car, NOW!'

We didn't need telling twice and neither did Rocky. He led us all back to the car and jumped straight in. Dad locked the doors and roared off down the track in a cloud of dust, the noise of the engine drowning out Big Mick's shouting and cursing.

It wasn't till we were back on the main road that my

legs stopped shaking and my heart stopped racing.

'Were you going to call the police, Dad?' I asked.

'Might have done,' he replied.

'But were you really?' Darren asked.

'Like I told you, I might have done,' Dad answered, 'except the phone was dead. I couldn't even get a signal!'

I was shocked at first, but Darren started to giggle, then Dad joined in and soon I couldn't help laughing as well. Rocky stood up, with his head close to Dad's, so he could get a better look out the windscreen as we headed home.

CHAPTER 10

We soon stopped laughing when we heard Dad's mobile ring. He passed it over to me.

Oh no! 'It's Mum!' I said, looking at the caller ID. I'd forgotten all about Mum. By now, she'd have got back from work and found the house empty.

'Answer it, Anna,' Dad said, 'but don't tell her about Rocky just yet, please.'

'Hi Mum,' I said reluctantly.

'Where on earth are you? It's nearly six o'clock! Is your Dad there? Is Darren with you? I've been ringing you for ages, but the phone was turned off!' She sounded desperate.

'Everything's fine, Mum,' I replied, glaring at Dad. 'We're all here and on our way home.'

'I've been worried sick! Where've you been? Have you got rid of that dog?'

'We took Rocky back … it was miles away…' I was trying to think of what to say, without telling any lies.

Of course, Mum knew straight away something was wrong. 'Anna, what's going on? Let me speak to your Dad!' she demanded.

Dad shook his head frantically and pointed at the steering wheel.

'Dad can't talk because he's driving,' I said quickly.

'Anna, tell Dad to pull over and answer this phone, now!' Mum's voice had gone all cold.

'Oh dear, the battery's run out! Have to go, talk to you later.' I cut Mum off.

'You are in so much trouble, Anna, telling Mum a whopper like that,' Darren piped up. He always likes it when I do something wrong.

'That's enough of that, Darren! I'll tell Mum it was my fault.' Dad was sticking up for me! 'Sorry I dropped you in it, Anna. I turned the phone on at Big Mick's place and forgot to turn it off again.'

So now Dad had even more explaining to do. For a while, I'd forgotten about what would happen at home, because rescuing Rocky was so important. Now we had to face the consequences.

'Shall we come and visit you when you're at Gran's?' asked Darren.

'Whatever are you talking about now?' said Dad.

'Anna said if you got in any more trouble you'd have to go and live at Gran's,' Darren went on. Trust

Darren to tell Dad – he can never keep his mouth shut about anything.

'Well, I don't know where Anna got that from,' Dad told him firmly, 'but I promise you I'm not going anywhere and neither is Rocky. Your Mum will understand, as soon as I explain everything.'

Where did Dad get these ideas from? I knew Mum wasn't going to listen to him, not after what he'd done. Hot tears began burning my eyes, and I tried to blink them away before anyone noticed. It felt like we only had a few minutes left before our whole lives changed – and Dad couldn't even see it.

When we pulled up outside the house, Mum was looking through the window. She came rushing out the door before Dad had turned off the engine.

'Don't say a word; leave this to me,' Dad muttered, getting out the car.

'Whatever took you so long? What do you think you're doing – going out all day with your phone turned off? And taking the kids without telling me!' Mum started in straight away.

'Sorry, love, I didn't mean …' Dad began, but he didn't get any further.

Mum had seen Rocky. For a moment she was speechless, then, 'Anna, Darren, go to your rooms, please.'

Mum was sending us out of the way, so this was really bad. I shut my bedroom door, then opened it quietly again so I could creep out on the landing and listen.

'What on earth's going on, Pete?' I heard Mum say. She was furious, although she was keeping her voice down so the neighbours wouldn't hear. 'I told you to get rid of that dog!'

'Come inside for a minute, love, and I'll tell you,' Dad replied. He led Mum into the hall, but left the front door open for Rocky to put his head round.

'You haven't got it have you?' Mum could shout now she was indoors. 'You haven't got the hundred pounds!'

'Come on, Jo, give me a chance to explain …'

'I knew it! I've been stacking shelves all day in that rotten supermarket while you've been up to goodness knows what! And taking the kids as well!'

Upstairs, Darren came out of his room and joined me. 'Has Dad sorted it out yet?' he whispered.

I shook my head. I wanted to cover my ears, so I wouldn't have to hear the rest of it, but at the same time I had to keep listening.

'I told you to take that lousy dog back, but you can't even do a simple thing like that!' Mum yelled.

I knew what would happen next. Dad was going to give up and clear off down the pub, like he always does. So I was really surprised when I heard him shout back.

'Just listen a minute, Jo, will you?'

'Don't you dare shout at me!' Mum got even angrier.

'I'm not shouting!' Dad lowered his voice, 'I'm trying to tell you what happened.'

Mum seemed surprised Dad wasn't walking away as well, because she stopped yelling.

'I want you to hear my side of it, please,' Dad went on.

'All right then,' Mum said, 'I'm listening, but don't you dare give me any more of your stupid excuses.'

Darren grabbed hold of my arm so tightly I had to bite my lip to stop myself calling out. Was there any chance Dad might talk Mum round?

'I wasn't going to take the dog back at first …' Dad started.

'There, I told you so!' Mum interrupted.

But Dad just carried on. 'Thought I'd get him a race – prove to you I could make us a bit of money for once. Only I got it all wrong as usual: Rocky can't run any more because he broke his leg. So I found the bloke who sold him to me. But when I saw how he treated the poor dog, I couldn't leave him there to be kicked and beaten. Not for a thousand pounds.'

I'd never heard Dad be so serious about anything before, and neither had Mum. He'd really got her listening now – and he still hadn't finished.

'I was wrong to spend the money without asking you, Jo, and I'm sorry about that, but I'm not sorry for bringing Rocky home. I bought him in the first place, so it's my job to see he's all right.'

I could see Mum standing there, open-mouthed. For once, she didn't seem to know what to say.

'And I'll pay that money back, Jo, every penny – I promise,' Dad finished. Then he turned to where Rocky was waiting. 'Come on, boy, let's get you settled. And there'll be no waking anybody up tonight, because I'm staying with you.'

Darren and I ran into my bedroom. We watched Dad walk down to the shed with Rocky so close beside him it looked like they were glued together.

CHAPTER 11

'You two can come down now,' Mum called up the stairs. 'I know you've been listening.'

Darren went charging into the kitchen. 'Mum, you should've seen Dad today! He was amazing! There was this horrible man who was going to kill Rocky and he was right in the middle of nowhere, like living in a rubbish dump and he was shouting at us and waving this big metal thing and Dad wouldn't let him hit Rocky, not even for tons of money!'

'Is that right?' said Mum.

'And this man said clear off and he was going to hit Rocky as much as he liked but Dad told him to stop or else …'

'Have you had anything to eat?' asked Mum.

That was the only question that could have possibly shut Darren up. 'No we haven't – I'm starving,' he remembered.

How could Darren think about food at a time

like this? I was sure I'd choke if I tried to swallow anything.

'I made some pasta bake – it only needs heating up,' Mum said.

Mum didn't mention Dad or Rocky and she didn't ask us any questions either. She just started banging plates around. I trailed after her, desperate to find out what she was going to do.

'Mum …' I tried.

'Put some glasses out, please Anna,' she said. I noticed she hadn't laid a place for Dad.

'Mum, please …'

'And when you've finished your tea, you can get on with your homework.'

Mum wasn't listening to me again! It was like she didn't care about how I was feeling anymore. I wished she'd have a good shout or something – at least that would be better than freezing me out like this.

'I've got some things to do,' Mum said, when Darren and I were eating. She still had that cold voice, like she was talking to strangers. 'I want both of you in bed early for school tomorrow. And you're to stay away from that dog!' Then she walked off upstairs.

Darren shovelled his food away and than disappeared to go on the computer. He didn't seem bothered that Mum was acting strangely or that she hadn't made it up with Dad. But there again, if the house fell down around him, I don't expect Darren would notice that either. I wished I could be like him sometimes.

I did the washing up and went up to my room. I tried to do my maths, but all the numbers kept swimming around in my head. I could see the shed from where I was sitting, although I didn't dare go and see how Dad and Rocky were doing, not after what Mum had said.

Perhaps I was making too much fuss. Lots of my friends' dads don't live with them and they still get to see each other. Yasmin says it's great, because she's got her own room in two different houses and double the amount of toys. And Ellen says it's better than all the arguing. Gran's isn't too far away, after all, and maybe Dad could get a nice flat of his own some time, although I don't know how he'd ever manage to look after himself.

I was trying hard to cheer myself up, but it didn't work. It only made me realise how much I would miss Dad if he wasn't there. Then I got this big panicky feeling, like an enormous wave washing over me. I had to find out what Mum was going to do, before it dragged me under.

I plucked up all my courage and walked across the landing to Mum and Dad's bedroom and went straight in. I got a terrible shock. The wardrobe door was wide open and our old suitcase was on the bed. Mum was holding a pile of Dad's shirts.

'What are you doing, Mum?' I gasped, as if it wasn't obvious.

'Anna!' she said, all surprised. 'Go back to your room!'

'But you can't, you mustn't!' I sobbed and now I was crying too hard to stop.

Mum could see how upset I was. She put her arms round me and we sat on the bed together. She was being kind at last, but it only made me cry more. 'Don't worry, love, everything will be OK,' she said, hugging me tight.

I hate it when adults say that. It's like the biggest lie in the universe and they expect you to fall for it.

'But Dad tried to tell you, he tried to explain ...' I began.

'Yes, he did, but that's just not good enough anymore, love.'

'And I tried to tell you as well, but you didn't listen – you never listen to me!'

Mum sighed. 'All right, Anna, I'm listening now.'

This was my one chance. I know Dad had made a lot of mistakes, but in the end he'd only tried to help Rocky. Now I had to convince Mum.

I took a deep breath. 'Dad didn't tell you everything,' I said, 'and Darren wasn't altogether right about what happened,' I said.

'I never imagined he was,' Mum said.

'But he wasn't all wrong either,' I went on. 'Rocky's

61

owner *was* a horrible man and he *was* cruel to Rocky. It was awful! But Dad stood up to him – he really did. He saved Rocky's life, even though he knew how mad you'd be when we got home!'

Mum went all quiet. 'Am I really as scary at that?' she asked.

'Yes, you are and you frighten me sometimes!' I blurted out without thinking. I saw how hurt Mum looked and I wished I could take the words back. 'But you don't mean to be scary, it's only because you get so fed up,' I tried to explain.

Mum didn't say anything for ages. Now I'd only gone and made things worse.

'You believe your Dad did the right thing, bringing that dog back here, don't you, Anna?' she asked me finally.

'I know he did,' I told her, 'and I know something else as well – if you'd been there, you'd have told him to do it!'

It seemed hours before Mum spoke again, though it was probably only a minute. 'Thank you, love, and I'm sorry for not listening to you before. Now, you need to get to sleep, but I will think about everything you said – I promise.'

That was the best I could hope for right then. I kissed Mum goodnight and went back to my room.

CHAPTER 12

Next morning, as soon as I heard Mum go downstairs, I tiptoed into her bedroom. Dad's clothes were hanging in the wardrobe and the suitcase was back in its usual place. I breathed a huge sigh of relief: so Mum hadn't sent Dad packing after all.

Mum was getting breakfast ready. Her eyes were red and she looked like she hadn't had much sleep, but she smiled when she saw me and gave me a long hug. Neither of us said anything about last night, I think we were both too worn out.

The house was very quiet for a Monday morning. Mum wasn't yelling at Darren to get out of bed or he'd be late, like she usually does.

'Darren should be up by now,' I said.

'Oh, he's gone to school already,' Mum replied, putting toast and a cup of tea on the table. 'Don't know what's got into him this morning.'

Neither did I: Darren never leaves the house before

me.

It only takes about fifteen minutes to walk to school, but I was so tired after the weekend my feet dragged along. I could see my best friends, Manjit and Alisha, waiting at the gate. They were waving excitedly and shouting at me to hurry up.

'Quick, Anna,' Manjit said when I arrived, 'you've got to tell us all about yesterday! Weren't you terrified? Wasn't your Dad cool!'

I guessed straight away how they knew what had happened. So this was why Darren had been in such a hurry to get to school.

'Well, it was a bit scary,' I began.

'Oh, come on, Anna!' said Alisha. 'Don't be so modest! Darren's already told us about how you rescued that poor dog and how your Dad stood up to that huge man.'

'His *name* was Big Mick, but actually he wasn't very …' I tried, but they weren't listening.

'And how your Dad and this man, they nearly got into a fight, but then your Dad scared him off!' Alisha carried on.

I looked round the playground and spotted Darren almost hidden by a crowd of kids hanging on to his every word.

'I think Darren might have exaggerated a bit …' I began.

Then I saw Marcus Harding and his gang push their

way to the front of Darren's group. They were the ones who'd been laughing at Rocky in the park, when Dad first brought him home. I thought they were going to cause trouble, but instead they started listening open-mouthed to whatever tale Darren was telling.

At that moment the bell went. For once I was glad when the teacher told us to stop talking and line up. I wouldn't need to say anything while we were in class and I could sort Darren out at break time.

It was hard to concentrate in Literacy. Every time Miss Knowler's back was turned, some of the boys kept whispering and pointing in my direction.

'Anna Stephenson, I asked you twice for an example of a persuasive text,' Miss Know-All said sharply. I hadn't even heard the question.

There were a few giggles, which the teacher squashed with one of her fierce looks. 'Can anyone else tell me?' she continued.

Jasbir put his hand up. 'I know one, Miss!' he called out.

'Very well, Jasbir,' Miss Knowles sighed.

'*Give us back our dog right now, or I'll give you a thump!* That's a good bit of persuasion, isn't it, Miss?'

Everybody, except for me, collapsed in a laughing fit.

Miss Know-It-All didn't think it was funny. 'I can't understand what's got into you all this morning, but if I speak to anyone again, there'll be a detention for the whole class.'

She kept us working nearly all the way through break, then there was Numeracy, so it was lunchtime before I had a chance to find Darren. He's in the year below me and I finally spotted him across the playground. I managed to shake Manjit and Alisha off by telling them I was going to the toilet. That gave me about five minutes.

'Don't you know everybody's talking about us?' I said angrily, as I caught up with him.

'That's right!' Darren actually sounded pleased with himself.

'But if you had to tell everyone, why did you have to make such a story out of it?' I demanded.

Before he could reply, Marcus Harding walked over and butted in. 'Fancy a game of football?' he asked.

Darren looked round to see who he was talking to. 'Who, me?' He was gobsmacked. Playing football with Marcus and his crew was Darren's all time, greatest wish come true.

'No, yer big sister, who d'yer think? Want to or not?'

'Wicked!' Darren said, and ran off.

Then some of the girls from my class found me and came running over. They had loads of questions they wanted to ask.

'Is Rocky all right?'

'What did your Dad do when that horrible man hit Rocky?'

'How did you get away?'

'Did he chase after you?'

'We think your Dad's a real hero, don't we?' added Alisha, and all the others agreed.

'Look,' I began, 'it was scary, but I think what Darren's told you is …'

Then I looked over to where Darren was playing football. I could hear him laughing and shouting with the other boys. He was having such a good time, I couldn't bring myself to spoil things for him. Perhaps he had exaggerated a bit, but he hadn't really made anything up and it *was* a good story.

'OK, then, everybody listen,' I said, 'here's what happened. It was exactly like Darren said …'

Dad and Rocky had made Darren the most popular boy in the school – at least for today. So perhaps that did make Dad a bit of a hero after all.

CHAPTER 13

I was glad it had been a busy day at school. I'd spent so long sorting Darren out and answering questions about Rocky, I hadn't once thought about Mum and Dad. But as soon as I started walking home, I felt all the worries closing in on me again, like a big cloud growing darker and heavier the nearer I got to our front door. I almost didn't want to put my key in the lock – it felt better to stay outside than have to go in and face any more troubles.

Mum was home from work before me. 'Hello, love, how was school?' she asked. I was glad to see she didn't look so sad or angry.

There was a lot of banging coming from the back garden. 'That's your Dad; he's been out there all day,' Mum said, but not in the cross, grumbly voice I expected.

So Dad was still here! And Mum was talking about him! I could feel the horrible black cloud starting to get a bit lighter.

There was one thing I wanted to do so much. I knew Mum had told me not to, but I had to ask. 'Mum,' I said slowly, 'can I go and see Rocky? Please?'

I thought she'd be cross, but instead she only gave a big sigh. 'Oh, all right then, but not for long – you've got homework to do.'

As soon as I ran out the back door, I saw what all the noise was about. Dad was building a wooden fence round part of the lawn in front of the shed. Rocky was lying close by, stretched out in a patch of sunshine and I went over to stroke him.

'Hello there, love,' Dad stopped hammering when he saw me. 'I'm making a safe place for Rocky.'

The fence was over a metre high with a gate so we could get in and out easily. 'Rocky's got his own bit of garden and he can go in the shed when he wants,' Dad explained. 'I got all this stuff from the tip – didn't cost me a penny!'

I was impressed. 'You're doing a great job, Dad,' I said and I meant every word. I'd never known him do anything like this before – there were always too many good programmes to watch on the TV, or mates to see down the pub.

Then we heard a clattering noise on the other side of the fence. It was Old Wilf from next-door climbing onto his chair to see what we were doing.

'You keeping that dog?' he snarled.

'And good afternoon to you too, Wilf,' said Dad pleasantly.

'I said, you keeping that dog?' Old Wilf repeated.

'We certainly are,' Dad replied. 'Wilf, meet Rocky.'

'Then make sure you keep him quiet – I didn't fight a World War just to be woken up by somebody's dog,' grumbled Wilf.

Dad rolled his eyes at me and mouthed, 'Daft old stick.' Then he winked and said out loud, 'Wilf, I can hear those kids throwing stones at your front door again!'

That soon got Old Wilf moving. 'Perishing hooligans! I'll get yer!' he shouted, scrambling down.

'Good thinking, Dad,' I smiled. 'But what's Mum say about this?'

'She hasn't said anything,' said Dad, meaning they still weren't talking. 'I don't think she minds though – I put those shelves up in the kitchen for her first.'

Whatever had come over Dad today? Mum had only been waiting about five years for him to do that job.

'Right, that's done,' said Dad, hammering in the last nail, 'now I won't have to stay down here with Rocky all the time. I'll even be able to sleep back in the house – if your Mum lets me in, of course.'

Dad sounded hopeful, but he hadn't seen Mum

packing his suitcase last night.

'But how are you going to stop Rocky howling, like he did at the weekend? I asked.

'I already thought of that,' Dad smiled. 'Rocky's like you, when you were little.'

I didn't go for that idea: I'm nothing like a greyhound.

Dad started to explain. 'When you were a baby and Mum went to work and I was looking after you, every time she left, you cried and cried. So Mum gave you one of her scarves. After that, whenever she went out, you cuddled her scarf and stopped crying.'

I still didn't get it.

'So I thought: if I left Rocky something of mine – like this,' Dad took off his old, sweaty T-shirt and put it on the ground, 'he'd think a bit of me was still with him. Come on, let's see if it works.'

We crept through the new gate and hid behind the shed, peering round to see what Rocky would do. It didn't take long for him to notice Dad was missing. First Rocky tried to follow Dad, but he couldn't get past the fence.

'He's getting anxious. We shouldn't leave him!' I said.

'Give him one more minute,' Dad persuaded me.

Rocky was pacing nervously up and down, when he came across Dad's T-shirt. He pushed it with his nose a few times. Then, amazingly, he lay down, put his head on it and went straight to sleep.

'It works!' Dad shouted and we gave each other a high five.

'You're brilliant, Dad!' I said.

'Absolutely brilliant!' Dad joked. 'If only your Mum knew it!'

As if she'd heard us, Mum started banging on the kitchen window.

'Go on in, love,' said Dad. 'Oh, and I nearly forgot – here's your money back. Sorry, Anna, I shouldn't have asked you for it in the first place.' Dad held out the cash from my moneybox, which he'd borrowed yesterday.

'It's all right, Dad. Rocky needs some stuff, so get him sorted and you can pay me back later.' Those new jeans didn't seem very important right then.

Inside, Darren was home. He was in the middle of telling Mum another endless story about his big moment at school. I don't think he'd stopped for breath yet.

'... and I got to play football with Marcus Harding! And he says I can play again tomorrow and he thinks it's wicked having Rocky and he wants to come round and see him! Can he, please, Mum? Can Marcus come round?'

As if that was going to happen! Marcus Harding's got the attention span of a gnat. Tomorrow he'll have forgotten all about Darren and Rocky and taken up with some other kid for five minutes.

Fortunately Mum didn't have to answer, because Darren spotted Rocky's new pen out of the window.

'Wow! Wicked! Did Dad do that? Is Dad going to sleep in the shed all the time, Mum? I think that's dead cool. Can I sleep in the shed as well?'

'No and no!' said Mum. 'You sleep here where I can see you – and Dad …' Mum looked at me, 'well, I suppose, Dad can always sleep on the settee.'

Now *that* was brilliant!! I ran out to tell him, before Mum could change her mind.

CHAPTER 14

Dad and Rocky were both missing when I got home the next day. It was around five o'clock when the car pulled up and Dad appeared, carrying loads of plastic bags.

'Hiya!' Dad called out cheerfully, dumping his shopping on the table.

'Been up town for a few things Rocky needs,' he explained. He went to give Mum a kiss, but she turned her face away.

Darren can hear the rustle of a carrier bag a mile off and came in the kitchen to see if there was anything for him. He unpacked a dog brush, two new bowls for food and water and a load of tins of dog food and packets of dry biscuit.

'This is gross!' Darren complained, looking at the pictures on the labels.

'*Real meat and gravy*,' read Dad, 'sounds delicious – why don't we have some for tea? Go on, Darren, fetch a plate – you'd look good with *a glossy coat and wet nose.*'

Dad started to chase Darren round the table till Mum told them to get from under her feet.

'Now come on out and see the best thing!' Dad told us.

Rocky was waiting patiently by the back door. He was wearing a new, bright pink collar and Dad clipped on a matching lead.

'Look at Rocky now! Isn't he a smart boy!' exclaimed Dad.

'It's great, Dad,' I said.

'Pink's a bit girlie though,' said Darren.

'Rocky doesn't mind about that, do you boy?' said Dad. 'He's not afraid to show his feminine side. Besides, they were cheap off the market. Now, I've got some news …'

Mum didn't give Dad a chance to finish. She'd been looking angrier and angrier as she saw all the things he'd bought.

'So there's more money you haven't got, wasted on that stupid dog,' she finally snapped.

Another big row was coming, I knew it. And it was my money Dad had spent, from the twenty pounds he'd borrowed, but I didn't dare let on.

'Come on, Jo,' Dad said, 'Rocky's got to eat.'

'So have we, but you never bother about that!' she shouted. 'Who's going to be the one paying for all this stuff from now on?'

'Well, actually …' Dad said, but Mum wasn't listening.

'Have you any idea what it costs to keep a dog?'

'I know, love, and that's why …'

'And I've got the gas and electric due and no sign of that hundred pounds you owe me!'

'I promised I'd pay you back, so today …'

'Big words don't pay the bills, Pete, as I keep telling you!'

'I GOT A JOB!' Dad shouted.

There was total silence. Even Mum was lost for words.

'What did you just say?' she asked eventually.

'I've been trying to tell you – I got a job. They're short-handed at that new building site behind the bus station and they're taking me on for a month,' Dad explained.

'Every day?' Mum still seemed stunned.

'Starting tomorrow,' said Dad.

I didn't know what to say either, it was so hard to believe. Dad does all sorts of jobs (when he feels like it), but they never involve turning up every day. And they've never lasted more than a week before.

'Come on, somebody, say something!' laughed Dad.

'It's not a joke is it, Dad?' I asked.

'No, love, I'm dead serious. I made your Mum

some promises – and Rocky too – and I'm going to keep them.'

I waited for Mum to make some nasty comment, but she didn't. At least Dad was trying, just like he said he would, and I hoped she'd seen it as well.

'I bet you've got to wear one of those special hats and orange jackets, like the builders who did our new school hall,' said Darren. 'They're well cool.'

'You're right,' said Dad.

'And drink loads of tea.'

'That's the best bit,' agreed Dad.

'So there's one part of the job you'll be good at,' put in Mum. But she didn't say it in a horrible way – she was actually smiling.

Dad looked so pleased she'd been nice, I wanted to give him a hug – and I did.

'Right, now,' Dad went on, 'there's no use putting a nice new collar on a filthy dog, so Rocky's in for a big treat. Time to give him a bath! Anyone want to help?'

'Yeah!' said Darren straight away.

I looked at Mum. 'Is it all right?'

'Go on, both of you,' she said straight away, 'give your Dad some help. He needs to save his strength for work tomorrow.'

CHAPTER 15

We filled all the buckets and saucepans we could find with warm water and carried them down the garden. I was practically running along, I felt so excited. Dad was keeping all the promises he'd made about Rocky, but in a bigger way than I'd ever imagined he would. And looking after Rocky meant that things were getting better at home, so it was like Dad was taking care of me and Darren as well.

The only one who wasn't pleased was Rocky. He must have guessed we were up to something, as he kept backing away until he was right up against the shed and couldn't go any further. His head went down and he stood there, shaking.

'He's scared we're going to hurt him,' I said.

'No, he just hates baths as much as I do,' said Darren.

Dad knelt down in front of Rocky and stroked his head, talking to him all the time in a calm voice. 'I'll have to hold him,' he whispered to us, 'while you two get him washed.'

'Hang on, Dad, I've got a good idea,' Darren said.

He went and fetched the watering can. Then he tipped the warm water in and poured it carefully over Rocky's back.

'Great!' laughed Dad. 'Rocky's got his own power shower! Perhaps if we keep watering him he'll grow into a Great Dane!'

Dad held on, but Rocky kept twisting and turning so much that soon he was soaking wet as well. 'Quick, Anna, rub some soap in while I've still got him,' Dad told me.

'But this is washing up liquid!' I said, picking up the bottle.

'It says on the tele: *cleans up all known dirt and good for sensitive skin*,' Dad replied.

There was no time to argue, so I squirted a bit onto Rocky's back and rubbed till he'd nearly disappeared under a cloud of foam.

'Look at the colour of the water, it's disgusting!' exclaimed Darren, showering the soap off with the watering can.

Finally, Rocky managed to wriggle free and shook himself all over, spraying the three of us with water. I threw a towel round him and gave him a good rub. Now all the dirt had gone, Rocky looked sparkling white for the first time. But you could also see the patches where his coat had fallen out more clearly. The tops of his hind legs were almost completely bare, making them look like a pair of giant chicken drumsticks.

When Rocky was dry, Darren and I took it in turns to brush him. At last we'd found something that Rocky really enjoyed – apart from eating and sleeping – and wasn't scared of. He stood there, perfectly calm and still, just turning his head to look at us whenever we stopped, like he was telling us to keep going.

There was the usual clattering and banging sounds as Old Wilf appeared over the fence.

'You going to race that dog?' he asked, in his snarly way.

'No chance!' replied Dad. 'Rocky's retired.'

'Besides, he can't run,' added Darren.

'Can't run? Can't run?' Wilf repeated and he started to make a strange, gurgling sound. I thought we were going to have to run for help, before I realised he was laughing.

'What you talking about – can't run? Don't you know nothing about greyhounds? Never seen a greyhound in my life what can't run,' Old Wilf went on.

'But he's broken his leg,' I explained, 'look – that one at the back.'

'Take more than a broken leg to stop a greyhound.'

'So you're the greyhound expert, are you now, Wilf?' said Dad with a smile.

'Knows a bit about them. More of a whippet man myself. Kept whippets for years in me younger days.'

'What's a whippet?' asked Darren.

'Like him, only smaller and nippier,' Wilf said. 'Where I come from, there was plenty of families kept whippets. Had our own races out on the hills. Useful dog to have is a whippet: get you a rabbit as often as not, and keeps your feet warm at night.'

Wilf had never told us anything about himself before. In fact, he'd never even spoken to us before, except when he wanted to grumble or complain about something. He had a far-away look on his face, as if he was remembering things he hadn't thought about for a long time. But he soon came back down to earth again.

'Like I told you before – make sure you keep him quiet!' he growled, back to his miserable old self. Then he clambered off his chair and disappeared behind the fence.

Dad put on his best Old Wilf voice: 'I didn't win a World War all by myself, just to be woken up by your dog,' and that set us all laughing.

Then Rocky stepped up close to me and started to push against my legs. I realised I was still holding the dog brush.

'Look at that, Anna!' exclaimed Dad. 'Rocky wants you to brush him again!'

I ran the brush along Rocky's coat and felt how soft and warm he was. I could see he would make a good hot water bottle on a cold winter's night. That made me think about Old Wilf and I wondered if he had anything to keep him warm now.

CHAPTER 16

It was strange having Dad go out to work. We were used to him coming and going when he felt like it; now he was getting up early and coming home at the same time every day. You'd think that would mean he wasn't around much, but in fact we saw him loads more than usual. He stayed at home in the evenings looking after Rocky, instead of rushing off down the pub. It made me realise just how little time he used to spend with us. I never thought Dad would stick with a job, even for a short while, but he did.

We got some time on our own at the end of the week. Mum was on the late shift and Darren had gone round to his friend Zack's for tea.

'I've got a special trip planned for Rocky tonight, Anna,' Dad told me. 'I'm taking him to the vet's; get him checked over properly. Hoped you'd come along as well.'

It sounded like a good idea, but I was sure Dad

hadn't thought it all through. 'Doesn't it cost loads of money to go to the vet's?' I asked.

'Yes, course it does, so we're going to the RSPCA,' said Dad. 'That's what the initials stand for, you know: the Right Spot for People who Can't Afford it.'

'Oh, come on, Dad! Everybody knows it's the Royal Society ...' I stopped when I saw Dad was laughing.

'Got you! You walked right into that one, Anna!' he joked.

'All right, you're one up – for now,' I agreed.

'One of the lads at work told me about it,' Dad went on. 'So I looked the number up in the phone book and gave them a ring. There's a clinic this evening; you just turn up.'

I was surprised Dad had found all this out by himself. He usually says he's too busy to bother with details and leaves everything like that to Mum.

'And while we're on our own, love, I wanted to say I know how much this means to you, keeping Rocky and working things out with Mum.'

I wasn't used to Dad talking to me like this, but the funny thing was, it didn't make me embarrassed, it gave me a nice warm feeling instead.

'And thanks, Anna, for sticking up for me and everything.'

'That's OK, Dad,' I told him, and it was. 'Come on, let's fetch Rocky.'

Rocky seemed really pleased about having another ride in the car. He got in straight away and went in his usual place: standing on the back seat looking over Dad's shoulder.

The RSPCA building was at the end of the high street. Rocky refused to get out of the car in a strange place, so Dad had to pick him up and carry him inside. We walked into a room with a small counter that said *Reception* and chairs all round the edge. It was like going to the doctor's, except the posters on the walls had pictures of animals instead of people with flu.

There was a lady behind the counter typing details into a computer. Her name badge said *Kate* and she had a smiley face.

'You're only just in time,' Kate told us, 'but I'm sure Miss Saunders will see you. Take a seat, please.'

Dad put Rocky on the floor and he hid under our chairs. We were the only people waiting, apart from one other woman on the opposite side of the room. She was wearing a pink velour tracksuit with a gap round her middle where a big roll of flab hung out. Her hair was bright yellow and pulled into a side ponytail. She had on those huge hoop earrings, which I think are cool, but Mum says are common. There was a bundle wrapped up in a blanket on her lap.

'Can I just take a few details, please?' Kate said to Dad.

He went up to the counter, giving me Rocky's lead

to hold.

'Have you been here before?' Kate asked.

'No, this is our first visit,' Dad replied.

'Name?'

'Mr Peter Stephenson.'

'No, not you – your dog!' Kate smiled.

'Oh sorry; Sheldon Rocket, but we call him Rocky.'

Kate took down lots more information, then Dad came and sat down again. He looked over at Tracksuit Lady and smiled, but she turned away, clutching her bundle more tightly.

We all jumped when a buzzer sounded.

'Snowy Mackenzie?' called out Kate. 'You can go in now.'

The woman got up and walked towards the door marked *Surgery*. I noticed the bundle she was holding start to twitch and squirm, so that she had trouble holding on to it. Suddenly the blanket fell off, revealing a white rabbit.

What happened next only lasted a few seconds, but it was like everything went into slow motion. Rocky shot out from under the chairs. I held on tightly to the lead, but he backed up, twisted his head and slipped straight out of his collar.

Tracksuit Lady's mouth fell open as she saw this greyhound making straight for her pet. She looked as if she was going to scream, but she couldn't get a sound out. At the same time, Dad dived full-length across the room, like a rugby player diving for a ball, and grabbed Rocky in the split-second before he got to the rabbit. His foot caught in a metal stand full of leaflets and the whole thing came crashing down.

Tracksuit Lady was furious. 'What do you think you're doing, letting a dangerous animal like that loose?' She started shouting about calling the police and loads more horrible things she wanted to do to Dad and Rocky.

Kate stepped in quickly. 'Get that dog under control!' she snapped at Dad.

Dad dragged Rocky away and held onto him with both hands. I ran forward to pick up the papers, which were all over the floor. Dad kept trying to say he was sorry and how he'd never seen Rocky do anything like that before.

'You should be locked up, frightening my Snowy like that, when he's come for the snip and all!' Tracksuit Lady yelled.

Eventually, Kate managed to calm her down and led her through the door to the vet. Rocky stood with his ears pricked, never once taking his eyes off the rabbit until it was out of sight. Then he sank back on the floor between Dad's legs.

'I really am sorry about what happened,' Dad apologised again.

'Don't worry; it wasn't all Rocky's fault,' said Kate.

'Small animals should be brought here in proper pet carriers, for their own safety. I had a word with Mrs M and she won't make a complaint – this time.'

'Whatever's got into you, Rocky-boy?' asked Dad, brushing himself down.

Rocky looked up at Dad, then rested his head on his front paws. He didn't seem to know what all the fuss was about. It was as if he was telling us he wasn't bothered: Snowy had got away, but he'd get him – next time.

CHAPTER 17

We jumped again when the buzzer went off for the second time.

'Rocky Stephenson!' called Kate. 'You can go in now.'

Dad tried to coax Rocky forward, but, with no Snowy in sight, he wasn't going anywhere. It was hard to believe that the dog trying to hide under chairs was the same one who'd just terrified a poor little rabbit.

Eventually Dad managed to drag Rocky along, his claws scrabbling on the floor, down a long corridor to a room at the back. It was a long way from the waiting room, so I hoped the vet hadn't heard all the commotion.

Miss Saunders was writing up some notes as we went in. She was a lot younger than I'd expected and very tall, with loads of red, curly hair. She had a white coat on and a pair of those half-glasses round her neck that old people wear. When she looked up and saw

Dad pulling Rocky through the door, I watched the smile freeze on her face.

'This is Rocky,' began Dad, 'I was hoping you'd …'

'Well, I can't, so just stop there,' the vet snapped.

Dad looked round to check we were in the right place. 'But you are a vet, aren't you?' he tried again.

'Yes, of course I'm a vet!' came the reply.

'And you take care of greyhounds, don't you?' Dad persisted.

'No, I certainly don't *take care* of greyhounds. I suggest you leave straight away.'

Now Dad really was confused. 'Is it because of the trouble in the waiting room? Or if it's a question of money …?'

'Money? Are you trying to offer me money? I don't believe it!' Miss Saunders interrupted furiously.

Dad looked at me in a bewildered way and I shrugged my shoulders. I didn't know what she was going on about either.

'I'm very happy to make a donation,' Dad tried again, reaching for his wallet.

This only made Miss Saunders lose her temper completely. 'How dare you come in here,' she yelled, her face as red as her hair, 'and bribe me to put down your dog!'

'Put Rocky down!' I panicked, grabbing Dad's arm.

'Put Rocky down!' Dad repeated. 'We came here to get our dog looked after and you want to put him down!' He bent over and scooped Rocky up. 'Come on, Anna, let's get out of here quick!'

We both turned for the door, but the vet got there before us.

'Wait a minute, Mr Stephenson,' she said, blocking our way, 'I think I've made a terrible mistake. Please give me a chance to explain.'

Dad looked at me and I nodded. He lifted Rocky gently onto the examination table, but didn't let go of him.

'I'm so sorry, Mr Stephenson, but I thought you wanted me to put your dog to sleep!' Miss Saunders said.

'Wherever did you get that idea?' Dad asked.

'Because I've been asked to do it before: to put greyhounds down when they can't run fast enough any more.'

'Does that really happen?' Dad asked. Neither of us could believe it!

'I'm afraid it does, sometimes,' Miss Saunders continued. 'Of course, the owners are supposed to find their dogs proper homes when they can't race. And lots of them really do look after their animals, but there will always be people who break the rules. The big problem is, there are far too many greyhounds to rehome and it's especially hard for the ones like

Rocky, who need special care.'

'What sort of care?' Dad asked. 'We want to get it right.'

'Well, some of them can be very nervous and anxious and they're not always used to being with people. It takes a lot of patience to take a dog like Rocky on.'

'He sort of took us on,' I said.

'Please can we start again? I'd be very happy to give him a thorough check-up – if you can trust me, that is,' Miss Saunders said.

Dad and I looked at Rocky. He was leaning against the vet with his eyes almost closed while she rubbed behind his ears.

'It looks like Rocky trusts you,' said Dad, 'so I'm sure Anna and I can as well.'

CHAPTER 18

Miss Saunders examined Rocky all over, talking to him gently the whole time. Rocky kept his eyes on Dad, but he didn't even flinch once. In fact, it was Dad who went 'Ouch!' when the vet lifted up Rocky's tail to take his temperature.

'This dog has been badly neglected, Mr Stephenson,' said Miss Saunders. 'Where did you say you found him?'

Dad told her all about Big Mick and how we'd brought Rocky home. 'I admit I thought he was just a way to make some quick money at first,' Dad said, 'but now I'm trying to take care of him.'

'Is Rocky all right?' I asked.

'He's very thin, but he'll soon gain weight now you're feeding him well. And he's got all these bare patches where his fur has fallen out; lots of them are sore and inflamed where he's been scratching. But he's very clean, although I'm not sure what you've been bathing him with.'

Dad went bright red. 'It said on the bottle: *kind to hands*,' he muttered.

'Washing up liquid isn't the best thing for dogs,' Miss Saunders sighed. 'I'll give you a special flea shampoo to stop the itching and help his skin heal. And what's this?' She pointed to Rocky's new pink collar.

'Dad bought that specially for Rocky,' I felt I had to stick up for him.

Miss Saunders rummaged around in a drawer until she found another collar with a funny shape. 'Greyhounds need a special collar like this one,' she explained. 'They can easily slip out of an ordinary collar and you don't want that to happen, do you?'

'No, no,' Dad muttered, 'we wouldn't want Rocky escaping.'

I hoped we could leave before she discovered what had happened in the waiting room.

'And Rocky needs an ID tag – that's the law, by the way.' Miss Saunders paused and peered at Dad over the top of her half-glasses. 'You don't really know much about dogs, do you, Mr Stephenson?'

'Look, Miss Saunders: first of all, it's Pete,' said Dad, 'and you're right, I don't know a lot about dogs yet, but I'm finding out. Tell us what he needs and I'll make sure he gets it.'

Miss Saunders smiled for the first time. 'Well then,

Pete, I think with a bit of TLC, Rocky will be fine.'

'That's great, isn't it Dad?' I was really pleased.

'But I am concerned about this leg,' said Miss Saunders, pointing to Rocky's bad leg. 'He's not putting his full weight on it and he's acting as if it's very sore.'

'He broke that leg racing,' Dad explained, 'but as long as he's not in any pain, we don't mind if he can't run.'

'Let me take an X-ray and find out a bit more.'

A few minutes later and the three of us were peering at the result.

'Here's the old injury,' said Miss Saunders, pointing to the grey shadows on the X-ray, 'but it's healed well. The bone's as good as new.'

'That's great news, isn't it?' asked Dad.

'It should be. Can you hold him please, while I have a closer look?' Miss Saunders felt carefully down Rocky's bad leg. 'All right, all right, boy,' she spoke reassuringly, 'I'm not going to hurt you.'

Poor Rocky began to whine and squirm, so it was all Dad could do to hold on to him.

'I can't find anything wrong with this leg,' the vet said, when she'd finished. 'There's no real reason why your dog shouldn't be able to run for miles.'

'So that's even better, isn't it?' I said.

'Yes, except that Rocky's leg is clearly troubling him. I've seen this before with other animals that have been badly treated. Rocky remembers that he hurt his leg; since then he's been too frightened to forget about the pain.'

'You mean, it's all in his mind?' asked Dad.

'A bit like that, yes,' replied Miss Saunders.

'So does he need a dog psychiatrist?' Dad wanted to know.

I liked Miss Saunders a lot because she didn't laugh. 'What he needs is what you're already giving him: a good home.'

'Then will his leg get better?' I asked.

'I can't promise you that,' Miss Saunders said. 'Sometimes the damage other people have done can't be repaired. It's all down to you now.'

It was upsetting to think that Rocky might always be as nervous and afraid as he was now. But it seemed to make Dad even more determined.

'We'll get you sorted, won't we Rocky-boy?' Dad said, lifting Rocky off the table. 'And thank you for all your help. Now how much do I owe you for the collar?'

'There's no charge. It's just a spare one I had lying around,' she replied.

'So are you a greyhound owner too, Miss Saunders?' asked Dad in surprise.

'What do you think happened to the two greyhounds I was asked to put down?' she laughed.

All that attention must have exhausted Rocky. He

fell fast asleep as soon as he got back in the car.

'That Miss Saunders was nice, once she got used to us, wasn't she, Dad?' I asked as we drove home.

'Very nice,' Dad agreed. 'I expect she fancied me.'

'Yes, she probably can't wait for you to come back and wreck her waiting room again,' I joked.

'She really gave Rocky a good going over, didn't she?' Dad went on. 'It was just like an MOT and a full service, but for dogs instead of cars.'

'That's right,' I said, 'that's why they call it an MOT test, because you have to get Marks Out of Ten.'

'You what?' said Dad. 'That's not what MOT means! Don't you know it stands for Ministry Of …'

'Got you, Dad! You walked right into that one!' I laughed.

CHAPTER 19

Dad was determined to put all of Miss Saunder's good advice into practice.

'She wants to see Rocky again in a few weeks,' he explained later to Darren and me, 'and I'm going to show her we really know how to look after this dog. Can I count on you two for some help?'

'Definitely!' I replied.

'All the way!' agreed Darren.

'Right then; here's the plan,' Dad said. 'There's feeding and walking and grooming and bathing.'

'We can help with all of that, Dad,' I said.

'And cleaning up – you know, after Rocky's done his business.'

Darren pulled a face. 'Yuck! No thanks!'

'We think that should be your job, Dad,' I told him, 'it can be a bonding experience for you and Rocky.'

'OK; so I get to be the pooper-scooper,' Dad smiled. 'But thanks a lot, kids, we're going to be a great team!'

Darren still seemed a bit disappointed. 'Aren't there any special jobs, Dad, that just me and Anna can do?'

Dad hardly hesitated. 'Of course there are! Err ... Darren – you can be in charge of the computer.'

'Wicked!' Darren was made up. 'I'm really good at that! What do you want me to do?'

'I think you should get on that Internet and, you know, sort of look things up.'

'Wicked!' repeated Darren. 'What sort of things shall I look up?'

'Well, stuff about greyhounds; sort of facts and things ...' Dad looked a bit lost, then he turned to me, 'and Anna, your special job is telling Darren what to look up.'

'OK, Dad,' I agreed.

'Rocky's got his own personal trainers now, hasn't he Dad?' said Darren.

'You're right, son, it'll be like going down the doggy-gym every day,' Dad laughed.

Rocky's healthy diet was no problem; he just ate everything we put in front of him as if it might be his last meal.

'Did you put in the sunflower oil?' asked Darren one evening. He began rifling through a pile of printouts he'd downloaded from some websites, which he seemed to be carrying round all the time. 'Only it says here: *a teaspoon added to a main meal will help give a glossy coat.'*

'Thanks, Darren, I nearly forgot,' Dad said.

Rocky's exercise plan wasn't so successful. It was very hard to persuade him to leave the garden and go for a walk, but Dad persevered. Strange notes started to appear on the calendar, where Dad recorded how far they'd got each day. At first, it was only FG (Front Gate), but soon Dad was writing WG (Wilf's Gate), CR (Crossed the Road), ES (End of Street), until at last they reached RTB!!! (Round the Block!!!).

Each time, Rocky came back looking totally exhausted as if he'd run a marathon, then slept for hours afterwards.

'You'd think he'd go for miles, wouldn't you,' Dad worried, 'after all his racing and everything?'

'It's all right, Dad,' said Darren, finding another piece of paper. *'FACT: greyhounds need very little exercise and twenty minutes twice a day is quite sufficient.'*

Trust Darren to go over the top since Dad had found him something to do. I could see we were all going to get fed up with greyhound facts very soon.

'That's good to know, son. But I'm trying to get him as far as the park – without having to carry him home,' Dad replied.

It wasn't long before we could see that all our efforts were beginning to pay off. Rocky was definitely improving. We knew he was putting on weight, because every other day we got to weigh him. We only had the bathroom scales and they were too small for Rocky to fit on, so first we weighed Dad, then we weighed Dad holding the dog and did the sums. Rocky looked as if he thought this was all very undignified, but he let us get on with it, as long as we were quick.

And the special shampoo was helping to heal the sore patches on his skin. Although Rocky never got used to being bathed, the time we spent brushing and grooming him seemed to make up for it.

Then, one evening after work, Dad was in the garden spending some time with Rocky like he always did, when suddenly I heard him shouting at the top of his voice, 'Jo! Anna! Darren! Get out here, quick!'

I thought something terrible had happened. All three of us raced outside.

'Whatever's the matter?' Mum called anxiously. She was still holding the potato she'd been peeling.

Old Wilf had heard Dad as well, and he came clattering up on his chair. 'Is it those young hooligans again? Let me get at them!' he yelled over the fence.

'Look! Look at Rocky!' Dad told us excitedly.

'Has he hurt himself, Dad? Is he all right?' asked Darren.

'No, son – he's great! He's brilliant!' Dad was beaming all over his face. 'Watch!' He knelt down and began to stroke Rocky and rub his ears. 'Look

101

what he's doing!'

We all stared. Slowly at first, then getting faster and stronger, Rocky's tail began to move; not from side to side like you'd expect a dog's tail to do, but round and round in bigger and bigger circles.

'Look at that,' Dad said proudly, 'he's wagging his tail!'

Darren and I let out a cheer. Even Old Wilf started to smile, before he remembered we could see him.

The only person not impressed was Mum. 'Is that it? Is that what we've run out here for?' she grumbled. 'You've frightened the life out of me and all because that stupid animal is wagging his tail?' She turned round and stamped off back into the house.

Dad didn't care. He looked like he couldn't have been more pleased if he'd won the lottery.

When I looked at the calendar next, Dad had circled today's date in thick, red pen and written the initials WHT in huge letters at the side. And it did feel like a red-letter day – the first time Rocky Wagged His Tail.

CHAPTER 20

One thing I hadn't been expecting was just how many people you get to know once you have a dog. Whenever we took Rocky for a walk, all sorts of people would stop and talk to us. Neighbours we'd never spoken to before, as well as complete strangers, made a big fuss of Rocky. They wanted to know all about him and how he was getting on. We got to recognise the other dog walkers too and we'd stop and chat about our animals while the dogs sniffed each other. It was a bit like being in a special club.

Old Wilf was often standing by his gate when we came back. He was always doing something, like sweeping up or putting out the bin, but I think he was really waiting for us to go past. Rocky always recognised Wilf and pulled on his lead, with his tail wagging, to go over to him.

Wilf usually found something to complain about. 'Keep that dog off my garden. I don't want him putting his leg up my geraniums,' he scolded. But that didn't stop him scratching Rocky in his favourite place behind the ears.

Old Wilf never asked about Rocky's progress, but Dad gave him all the details anyway. Wilf pretended not to listen, but you could tell he was hanging on to every word.

'Went back to the vet's for a check-up yesterday and she said this dog's doing great,' Dad told him proudly one day.

But Wilf always knew best. 'He'd do a lot better if you stopped molly-coddling him. A greyhound's a working dog and you lot're turning him into a pekin-flippin'-ese,' he grumbled.

When Dad saw Rocky wasn't nervous meeting new people any longer, he said it was OK for our friends to come round. Most days after school, somebody from mine or Darren's class would drop in to see Rocky. Mum didn't grumble, but she took extra care checking my homework and making sure I got everything finished before I spent any time with Rocky.

Each time the doorbell rang, Darren jumped up and ran to see who was there. He always looked disappointed. I knew he was waiting for one particular person, but Marcus Harding never came.

That went on through the half-term holiday, then, by the time we went back to school, the novelty had worn off and life settled down again. I didn't mind, as

I liked things being a bit quieter, but I think Darren missed not being the centre of attention any more.

We hadn't had any visitors for a while, when the doorbell went just as we were finishing tea.

'Who is it this time?' sighed Mum.

Darren had given up running to the door, so I said I'd go. I thought it was probably Alisha wanting some help with her maths homework.

There was a boy standing on the step. He had a baseball cap with a hoodie pulled over it, hiding his face.

'MUM!' I shouted nervously.

She came running out. 'Not today, thank you,' said Mum. She started to close the door, when I heard the boy mumble something.

Mum must have thought he was swearing at her, as she flung the door open and yelled, 'I beg your pardon?'

'I've come to see the dog,' said the boy, much louder. Then he looked up and I saw who it was.

'What's going on, Mum?' asked Darren, coming to find out what was happening. He recognised the boy straight away.

'Marcus! Mum, it's Marcus Harding!' cried Darren delightedly.

'I've come to see the dog,' Marcus repeated, in that sneery way he talks to grown ups.

Mum wasn't at all impressed. 'That's not how we

ask for anything in this house,' she told him.

At first, there was no reply, then I was amazed to hear Marcus mutter, 'I've come to see the dog – *please*.' I didn't think he even knew the word.

'Can he, Mum? Please, Mum? Can Marcus see Rocky? Please say he can!' burbled Darren, full of excitement.

'All right, then,' agreed Mum reluctantly. 'Come on in, Marcus.'

Marcus began to shuffle into the hall.

'Wait just a minute, though, please,' Mum hadn't finished yet. 'We don't wear caps in this house.'

'Mum!' Darren hissed in embarrassment.

I was certain Marcus would turn round and walk out, with plenty of his usual swearing thrown in. Instead I was astonished to see him pull his hoodie down, take off his cap and stuff it in his pocket.

Seeing Marcus Harding without his cap was a bit like seeing the Queen naked and just as much of a shock. All of a sudden, he didn't look so tough anymore.

I realised I was standing there with my mouth wide open when I heard Mum say, 'Anna, can you go with them, please?'

Neither Darren nor I liked that idea, but I realised Mum wanted someone to keep an eye on things. I knew how much having Marcus here meant to Darren, so I felt I had to go along with it, even if it meant standing around like a spare part.

The three of us trooped out into the garden and into Rocky's pen. Rocky was lying in a patch of late sunshine, but he got to his feet when he heard us and came over.

'Look, Rocky, here's my friend Marcus come to see you,' said Darren.

Marcus began to back away. 'He's a bit big, ain't he?' he mumbled.

'Don't worry,' Darren reassured him, 'he's big, but he's ever so gentle. He just wants to sniff you – that's his way of getting to know you.'

Rocky kept walking towards Marcus, who by now had his back against the fence. Whoever would have believed it? That big bully Marcus Harding was scared of a dog!

'Hold your hand out,' Darren explained patiently, 'he won't hurt you.'

Marcus couldn't get any further away. I saw him look around as if he was wondering whether to scramble over the fence and make a run for it. Then, very reluctantly, he put his hand out.

'That's great!' said Darren. 'Now keep still.'

'Is he gonna bite me?' asked Marcus.

'Never!' replied Darren. 'He just wants to be friends.'

Marcus's hand was shaking. He stood as still as a statue while Rocky sniffed it all over. Then he reached out his other hand and very gently began to stroke Rocky's head.

'Don't you like dogs, Marcus?' I couldn't help asking.

'Got bit by a Staffie once – still got the scars,' he replied.

'Rocky wouldn't hurt a fly,' said Darren. 'Do you want to brush him?'

'What me? Will he let me?' asked Marcus.

'Course he will,' Darren laughed, 'he loves it!'

Darren came back with the dog brush and showed Marcus how to groom Rocky. Then Marcus had a turn.

'Soft, ain't he – and warm.' Talk about stating the obvious! But Marcus sounded like he'd discovered something new.

'Look – he likes you!' said Darren, as Rocky closed his eyes and leant against Marcus's knees.

'Yeah, he does, I think he likes me!' repeated Marcus.

I couldn't believe it either. 'I wonder why?' I whispered to Darren, but he gave me a shove. Marcus was too busy going all soft over Rocky to have heard me.

'What's he eat? Where'd you walk him? How old's he?' Marcus had hundreds of questions for Darren.

I gave a big sigh; this was going to take a long time. Then I saw Mum wave to me from the kitchen window. She was telling me it was all right to come back inside and leave the boys to it.

CHAPTER 21

Things stayed very quiet at home. Dad was still sleeping on the settee, but there weren't any more rows. Mum and Dad were very polite to one other, especially when me and Darren were in the room. They talked about what we were doing at school and what we were having for tea and if it was going to rain. Although they'd stopped arguing, it seemed like they didn't have much else to say to each other.

But one thing remained the same; Mum didn't want anything to do with Rocky. She wouldn't go near him and she never even mentioned him, except to call him 'that dog'. It was like he didn't exist.

I meant not to say anything, but one night when Mum was tucking me up in bed, all the things I'd been thinking came rushing out.

'Dad's trying really hard, isn't he, Mum? He's going to work every day and he's taking good care of Rocky, like he said he would. I wish you were pleased about it,' I told her.

At first, Mum didn't answer and I began to wish I'd kept my big mouth shut. Then, I heard her say quietly, 'I've let Dad and Rocky both stay here, Anna, don't forget that.'

'But you act like Rocky's invisible!' I blurted out and felt tears sting the back of my eyes.

Mum gave me a hug. 'I can't do any more right now, Anna love,' she said, 'four weeks is such a short time and your Dad has made a lot of promises before.'

'I think it might be different this time,' I said.

'I know you do, love, and that's why I don't want to see you get hurt.'

I lay awake for ages after Mum had gone. It was so hard to think that looking after Rocky might turn out the same as Dad's other big ideas – something he'd soon get fed up with. And what would we all do if that happened?

Then, in no time, Dad's month at work was up. When I got back from school, Mum was bustling round the kitchen and Darren was hanging around instead of going off to play. Nobody mentioned it, but I could tell we were all waiting for Dad to come home.

I heard the car pull up, and next the back door opened. Dad looked surprised to see us all.

'Hi everyone,' he called, 'wasn't expecting a family meeting. Make us a cup of tea, will you Jo?' He sat down and put the bags he was carrying on the table. 'Glad you're all here, because I've got a few things to give out.'

'Presents! Great!' said Darren.

Mum and I looked at each other. Dad would have been paid off today and we knew how much he liked spending, when he had some money on him.

'Darren – this is for you; to say thanks for all your help with Rocky,' said Dad.

Darren was thrilled. 'The new DVD I wanted! Wicked! And it came from a real shop! It won't be all fuzzy and grey like the ones you buy us at the car boot sale. Thanks Dad!'

'Here, Anna, I think you can use these.' Dad passed me a New Look bag.

I was amazed when I took out a pair of those skinny jeans I'd been saving for. I didn't even think Dad knew my size. 'They're perfect! Thanks Dad – I've been wanting these for ages.'

There was a little note stuck on the label, which said: *TOP SECRET: LOOK IN BACK POCKET.* It was a twenty-pound note – Dad had paid back the money he'd borrowed. He saw me looking and winked.

'And I got a some treats for Rocky,' said Dad, handing Darren another carrier.

'What're these?' asked Darren, pulling a face. He held up a bag of dry, brown, triangular objects with a peculiar smell.

'Pigs' ears!' replied Dad. 'Dogs love them.'

He picked out two, held them on top of his head and started to chase Darren round the room, making grunting noises.

'Gerroff, Dad, they're gross!' Darren shrieked.

The presents were great and for once they didn't look like Dad had wasted his money.

'I didn't buy you anything, Jo,' Dad said to Mum, 'I thought you'd rather have this instead.' He pushed over an envelope. It was full of twenty-pound notes. 'There's the hundred pounds I took to buy Rocky, like I promised, and a bit more. It's all my wages, except for what I spent on the kids and Rocky.'

I thought Mum would be thrilled, but she wasn't.

'It's only a month's money, you know, Pete. This won't go far,' she said.

'No,' Dad replied, 'don't suppose it will; that's why I saw the boss today.'

'Oh yes, and what was that all about?' said Mum.

'He's asked me to stay on a bit – there's a new contract come in. Could be another three months, if I'm lucky.'

'And what did you say?' she asked.

'Told him I'd give it a go.'

Mum's mouth fell open in surprise. 'You're staying on? At the building site? You mean it?'

'Steady on, love,' Dad told her, 'it's only till something better turns up.'

113

'Pete Stephenson: the bread and dog food winner!' laughed Mum. 'I can't believe it!'

Neither could I, but it was the best present Dad could have brought home. For the first time, I let myself start to believe that perhaps things might get better for all of us, from now on.

CHAPTER 22

'Now there's one more surprise left, so wait for it!' announced Dad. 'No cooking for your Mum tonight, kids,' he announced, 'I'm taking her out!'

'Taking me out?' repeated Mum. 'But we never go out!'

'We are tonight. Get your posh frock on, Jo – I've booked us a table at that new Italian: the one with the dim lights and sexy music.' Dad grabbed Mum and began to do a smoochy dance round the kitchen, till she pushed him off.

'Give over, Pete!' Mum told him, but she was trying not to laugh.

'Yucko! Stop it, will you?' said Darren, pulling a face.

'What about Anna and Darren though? Who's going to look after them?' asked Mum.

'All taken care of, love,' replied Dad. 'You're

115

looking at the man who's thought of everything: I've asked Mum to baby-sit.'

'Oh no!' Darren and I both said together. We don't often agree, but the thought of an evening with Gran was one of the few things we felt the same about.

'She says she'll get their tea as well – give you a proper break,' Dad said.

'YUCKO!' That was me and Darren together.

We'd had Gran's teas before. Her idea of cooking is boil-in-the-bag fish with tinned potatoes and watery peas. I saw Mum hesitate. I knew she wouldn't go if we made a fuss, no matter how much she wanted to.

'Only joking, Mum!' I said, glaring at Darren. 'You go and have a great time.'

Darren scowled back, but at least he kept quiet.

Mum's face lit up and she ran upstairs to get ready. 'Nobody else in the bathroom for the next hour!' she called down. I can't remember when I'd last heard her sound so cheerful.

It's not that we don't like our Gran. She's very kind and nice to us; it's just she's so totally exhausting to be with. She's in her sixties, but tells everybody she's forty-nine. And she keeps trying to get us to call her 'Stella' instead of Gran. (Her real name's Susan, but she won't let anyone use it.) Last time she came to baby-sit, she made us stay up late playing cards and dancing to loud music.

It wasn't long before we heard the gate open and

someone shouting, 'COO-EE! COO-EE!' Why Gran can't ring the bell like other people, I'll never know.

I opened the door. Gran was wearing tight jeans with a shiny red shirt. She'd dyed her hair again and it had turned several shades of orange.

'Hello, Anna, sweetheart,' she called, jangling all her bracelets as she wrapped me in a big hug. 'How d'you like me new top?'

Gran did a twirl on the doorstep. She had one of those trendy sleeveless jackets on; the ones with lots of fake fur round the edges that teenagers wear.

'It's great, Gran,' I told her, with my fingers crossed.

'Not so much of this *Gran* lark, there's a good girl – you're making me feel old! I've got a lovely bit of cod for our tea.' She handed me an Iceland carrier bag. 'Now, I'll just nip round the back and see your new doggy.'

I'd forgotten Gran hadn't met Rocky. I watched her wobble off down the path on her high, spiky heels. That new jacket gave me the shivers; it looked like she had a small animal wrapped round her neck.

And then I suddenly remembered what had happened at the vet's.

'Dad!' I yelled, running through the house and out the back door. 'Come quick!'

'Who's a nice doggy, then? Who's a lovely boy?' Gran was calling to Rocky over the fence.

I needn't have worried: the fence would keep Rocky away until I got Gran indoors. Except it didn't. The instant he saw Gran, Rocky's ears went up. Then, without a moment's hesitation, he jumped right over the fence and made straight for her jacket.

'Help! Help!' Gran screamed. 'Get him off me!'

'Down, Rocky! Good boy, Rocky!' I yelled.

'What's going on?' said Dad, rushing outside.

Rocky was sniffing all round the furry bits of Gran's coat. He was very excited, but he was wagging his tail at the same time.

'Get him off!' screamed Gran again, flapping her hands in the air. 'He's attacking me!'

Rocky thought this was a great game. The more Gran flapped, the livelier he got. But you could see he was only playing. Obviously he could tell the difference between a real rabbit and a bit of fake fur.

'Stand still, Mum!' ordered Dad, grabbing Rocky by the collar and pulling him away. 'He won't hurt you. He's just being friendly.'

'Friendly? Friendly?' said Gran, when Dad had Rocky at a safe distance. 'He could have taken me arm off!'

'It's all right, really, Gran,' I tried to quieten her down, 'he just wants to get to know you.'

'Whatever's going on? Are you all right Sue-Stella?' Mum said, as she and Darren came running out.

'Did you see Rocky?' said Dad. 'He jumped the fence! Rocky jumped the fence!'

'Is that all you're bothered about, Peter, when your dog's just given me the fright of my life?' Gran demanded.

Eventually we got Gran indoors and managed to calm her down, although it took a couple of gin and tonics to convince her that Rocky was harmless. Dad must have made them strong, as she let Darren fetch a take-away for our tea and was snoring on the settee by ten o'clock.

I'd been asleep for ages when I heard Mum and Dad come in. It was the sound of them laughing that had woken me up. I heard both their footsteps on the stairs and their voices whispering on the landing, before their bedroom door closed quietly behind them.

CHAPTER 23

The next morning was the weekend. Darren was out at football practice and Dad and I were getting ready to take Rocky for his walk.

'Where are you off to this morning?' Mum asked. It was the first time she'd ever bothered to find out.

'We're going for the record today, aren't we Anna? It's the park and back, or I'm a pig's ear!' said Dad.

'I could do with some fresh air. I might come along,' said Mum.

Mum actually wanted to come for a walk with Rocky! I was so happy, I felt like jumping up and down.

Dad shut his eyes and pretended to collapse. 'I must have fainted for a minute,' he said to me, 'I thought I heard your Mum say she wanted to come with us.'

'Stop messing about, Pete, I told you I just need a breath of air,' Mum said sharply.

'Hurry up, Anna! Let's get Rocky – quick, before

she changes her mind! I'll have to mark this special event on the calendar!' Dad was making fun of Mum, but I could tell he was really, really pleased.

Rocky was waiting patiently in his pen. As soon as he saw Dad, he started wagging his tail and doing a little dance as if he was going to burst with excitement.

'Hello there, boy, hello Rocky,' said Dad, while Rocky acted as if it was the happiest moment of his life. 'Who's a good boy? Who's my best dog?'

'Whatever does that dog see in you, Pete?' said Mum.

I think she only meant it as a joke, but Dad still looked hurt.

'At least Rocky's always pleased to see me,' he said quietly. 'We all need somebody who thinks we're special.'

Dad's reply stopped me in my tracks and even Mum looked surprised. I was so used to Dad laughing and joking, I'd never stopped to think he might be unhappy sometimes, too.

'Shall I put Rocky's lead on, Dad?' I asked, trying to make things better.

'Right you are, love,' he said brightly, although he looked miserable.

I held the lead as the three of us set off. Rocky's pace was slow, especially as he liked to stop and sniff nearly everything in sight. Usually I don't mind, because Dad and I can find loads to chat about, but, with Mum along, none of us knew what to say. I was beginning to wish she hadn't bothered to come.

Then we walked through the park gates for the first time. Dad was so thrilled Rocky had got this far, all his sad thoughts seemed to vanish.

'Well done, Rocky! Well done!' he said over and over. 'This calls for a celebration: the ice-creams are on me!'

We went up to the van and Dad bought 99s for the three of us and an orange ice-lolly for Rocky. 'Don't tell that nice vet, will you, Anna?' he joked.

Then we found a bench to sit on. Rocky pushed in between us to reach the lolly Dad was holding and was soon covering his jeans in orange drips.

'What a mess!' said Mum. 'Here, give it me.'

She took the ice-lolly from Dad and held it while Rocky licked it down to the stick! Mum had never, ever done anything for Rocky before, and I wondered if this was her way of showing Dad she was sorry for upsetting him.

When Rocky had finished, he shuffled over and lay down on Mum's feet. It was the first time Mum'd let Rocky get near her. I expected her to push him away, but she let him stay there.

'Look at that!' laughed Dad. He sounded really surprised and pleased at the same time. 'And I thought Rocky only had eyes for me!'

'Don't worry, Pete – it's just cupboard love,' said Mum. 'That dog knows you're the one who takes care of him.'

'I'm just doing what I can,' said Dad.

'I think that's more than enough,' Mum told him.

'Maybe,' Dad said, 'but he's still a long way from the dog he used to be. It's hard to believe that poor old Rocky, who can hardly even walk to the park, was ever Sheldon Rocket, the champion greyhound.'

'You have to give him time,' said Mum.

I couldn't believe my ears: Mum and Dad were actually talking together! And not just about the weather or, *do you want a cup of tea?* but about things that really mattered.

'The vet did say he might run again, but I can't see it myself,' Dad went on.

'Perhaps Rocky doesn't mind, Dad,' I put in, 'perhaps he'd rather live with us than win races.'

'Anna's right, Pete,' Mum went on. 'Rocky's learned to make the best of things. We can't all have everything we want.'

'But we can still try to make things better, can't we?' replied Dad.

Then I knew Mum and Dad weren't just talking about Rocky; they were thinking about other stuff as well.

Suddenly Dad jumped up, as if things had got a bit too serious. 'Come on, Rocky's ready to walk back now,' he announced.

I kept quiet and walked behind them all the way home, hoping Mum and Dad might have some more to say to each other. Nothing happened till we were nearly there, when Dad turned to Mum and said, 'Thanks for coming with us today, Jo, and for giving Rocky some attention. It means a lot, you know.'

'That's all right,' she replied. 'It's been a bit like old times, hasn't it? We always used to take the kids to the park when they were little.'

'Do you remember how walking with Anna was as slow as walking with Rocky, because she had to stop and look at everything?' said Dad.

'And then Darren always tried to climb out of the pushchair ...' began Mum.

' ... so I ended up carrying him on my shoulders,' finished Dad.

'And then one week he was sick all in your hair ...'

They kept on like this all the way up the path. I took Rocky down the shed, but I turned round just in time to see Dad put his arm round Mum as they went indoors. And the best bit was that Mum didn't push him away.

CHAPTER 24

After that day in the park, Mum stopped pretending Rocky wasn't there and began to pay him some attention. It didn't happen all at once, of course, but gradually she seemed to come around to the idea that he was our dog.

It was Rocky himself who helped win Mum over. He'd never stopped trying to follow her, whenever she was in the garden, and he was always looking at her with his big, wet eyes, as if he was begging her to notice him.

'What's wrong with this stupid dog?' Mum used to say. 'He knows I don't like him, but he never leaves me alone.'

She didn't say that any more. Now, when Rocky stood by Mum, she stroked and patted him. And whenever Rocky saw Mum, his tail would go into a spin with all the excitement.

'Look how pleased Rocky is to see you, Jo!'

laughed Dad. 'He knew you liked him all along – you were just trying not to show it.'

'That stupid dog likes anyone who makes a fuss of him,' Mum grumbled.

Then, one evening, Dad was searching through the kitchen cupboards for some more tea bags, when he came across a plastic bag pushed right to the back.

'Jo? Whatever are these?' he said, taking out a box of dog biscuits.

Mum went bright red. 'Found them at work … the packet's broken … they were   only going to throw them away.'

I'd never known Mum get flustered like that about anything.

A big grin broke out on Dad's face. 'You've been giving these to Rocky, haven't you?' he laughed.

'Oh come on, Pete, it's no big deal, I didn't want to waste them, that's all,' said Mum.

'You'll be letting him come in the house next!' joked Dad.

I saw Mum's face go redder still.

'You've already done it, haven't you?' Dad guessed straight away.

'Don't make so much fuss, Pete. The dog's only been in the kitchen a few times, when I'm on my own in the day,' said Mum.

'Did you two hear that?' Dad turned to me and Darren. 'Your Mum's been making up to Rocky on the quiet! Now this I've got to see.' He ran out the back door to fetch Rocky.

Rocky walked straight in the kitchen and waited by Mum until she gave him a biscuit. Then he lay down under the table, as if he'd been doing it forever.

'YES!' shouted Dad, punching his fist in the air. Then he grabbed Darren and they did a dance round the table.

'Be serious, will you Pete?' Mum said, but she was laughing too.

'Rocky's a proper pet now, isn't he Dad?' said Darren.

'He's part of the family,' Dad agreed, putting his arms round Mum. 'That's right, isn't it, Jo?'

Mum hesitated and I held my breath.

'Yes, that's right,' she said, 'Rocky belongs to all of us.'

Later on, when we were watching the TV, someone left the kitchen door open. Rocky walked into the living room and lay down on the rug next to Dad. I thought Mum might throw him out, but, instead, it was like no one noticed anything different. Dad began to rub behind his ears and Mum moved her legs to make room for him as if he'd always been there.

I looked round at all of us and wished I could take a picture to capture that moment. We weren't doing anything special, but we were sitting together as if that was the best place to be. I remembered those adverts

I'd watched with smiling families getting excited about washing powder or gravy. I'd always wondered what it would feel like to be like that. Now I knew, only this was better, because it wasn't just getting our clothes clean that was making us happy.

That's when I felt a cold shiver run down my body. What if things didn't stay like this much longer? Dad's job was going to end soon and he might not want to work anymore. Then Mum would get angry and all the rows would start again.

More than anything, I wanted us to stay like we were in my special picture. If only I could find a way to make it happen.

CHAPTER 25

After Rocky jumped over the fence when Gran came to baby-sit, Dad got thinking again.

'Did you see what that dog did?' he asked. 'If he can jump like that, then his leg must be getting better!'

'Does that mean he'll run again, Dad?' asked Darren.

'Perhaps he will after all, son,' Dad replied.

Rocky's bad leg certainly was improving. It didn't tremble as much as it used to and he put his weight on it nearly all the time now.

'Come on, let's see if he can jump like that again,' Dad decided.

We went out in the garden and Dad propped up some sticks on the lawn for Rocky to jump over. Then he stood at one end calling to him, 'Come on, Rocky! Come on, Rocky!'

Rocky yawned. He gave Dad a look as if to say, 'You must be joking,' and lay down.

Dad wasn't ready to give up. 'I think he needs you to show him what to do,' he told Darren and me.

So we had to take turns jumping over the sticks, while Rocky lay and watched us. When that didn't work, we tried again, holding a pig's ear. That got Rocky moving. He wanted the treat all right, but, while we ran and jumped, he just walked round the side.

'What're you lot doing with that dog?' we heard a voice shout from over the fence. It was Old Wilf, who'd got up on his chair to see what was going on, as usual.

'We're getting him to jump,' said Dad

'Jump? Jump?' repeated Wilf. 'What's he want to jump for? He's a greyhound, not a kangaroo.'

'But he might be a hurdler. *FACT: greyhounds can race over three separate flights of hurdles,*' Darren recited.

'Thank you Professor Einstein,' replied Wilf. But he looked a bit put out: I don't think he'd expected Darren to know that.

'And he's already jumped over the fence,' I said.

'Well, go on then, let's see him do some of this hurdling.' Wilf leant on the fence as if he had all the time in the world.

It was a lot harder with Wilf watching. I was desperate for Rocky to prove he could do it, but, no matter how many times we tried, he didn't show the slightest interest in jumping over anything. Darren and I ended up exhausted, while Rocky had just walked up and down.

'Load of old rubbish,' said Wilf, disappearing into his own garden at last.

'Perhaps this is a bit too hard for Rocky,' Dad said.

That incident with Gran had got Dad's hopes up and I could see he was really disappointed, although he was doing his best to hide it.

'Never mind, Rocky-boy,' he said, 'we'll try another day.'

But we never did – I don't think Dad wanted to risk being let down again.

Darren didn't seem too bothered that he'd been running around for nothing. He was in a good mood every day lately, since Marcus Harding had come to see Rocky. As far as Darren was concerned, that was the most important thing in the whole universe.

After his first visit, Marcus kept coming back. Practically every day after school he'd turn up – or at least, that's what it seemed like to me. He was round our house so often it felt like we'd adopted him.

I kept waiting for the novelty to wear off, but it didn't happen. Marcus spent ages playing with Rocky or discussing greyhound facts with Darren. I didn't mind so much, because Rocky always gave Marcus a big welcome and loved the tons of attention he gave him.

The next time Marcus arrived, the two boys disappeared into Darren's room to play on the computer. Suddenly, they both came running downstairs.

'Look at this!' Darren announced excitedly. 'We Googled *Sheldon Rocket* and look what came up!'

Darren had printed out an old newspaper report. *'Rocket Wins the Challenge Cup',* said the headline, followed by a picture of three greyhounds crossing the finishing line.

'It's our Rocky!' Darren went on, pointing to the leader.

There was no mistaking Rocky. You could pick out those special markings – his one black leg and eye patch – clearly in the picture. But we'd never seen him like this before. This Rocky was racing past the winning post with all four legs off the ground, as if he was flying through the air.

'Would you believe it!' said Dad.

'It was Marcus's idea, wasn't it Marcus?' said Darren.

'Yeah,' replied Marcus.

'Tell them your other idea, Marcus,' suggested Darren.

'Yes, please tell us, Marcus,' said Mum, when nothing happened.

'Thought we could print some off. Put them round the house and shed, like, to remind him, like, about running and stuff,' explained Marcus.

I thought everyone had forgotten about Rocky running again, but it looked like Darren and Marcus were still working on it.

'That's a great idea,' said Mum.

'Because we all know how much Rocky enjoys a good read,' I put in.

'That's enough, Anna,' Mum glowered at me. 'Thank you, Marcus.'

'What do you think of this, Rocky?' said Dad, holding out the sheet of paper. 'Look who's here! That's you, that is!'

Rocky plodded over. He gave the printout a good sniff, then walked away when he discovered it wasn't something to eat.

'Thanks a lot boys,' said Dad, 'and Mum's right – it is a good idea. But I don't want you two getting your hopes up. Rocky's not a racing dog any more. He'll never run like that again.'

'Don't give up on him!' Marcus butted in.

He looked as astonished as we did, speaking up like that. I didn't even know he could talk in proper sentences.

'Go on, Marcus, say what you think,' said Mum.

'What I mean is, like, you never know, like, what anybody can do. Till you gives them a chance, like …'

It was hard for me to admit it, but I thought Marcus

might be right. Perhaps Rocky was going to do lots of things we didn't even know about yet.

All we had to do was carry on making sure we gave him that chance.

CHAPTER 26

The next Saturday, Dad was working an extra shift at the building site and Mum had gone shopping, so Darren and I were on dog duty in the garden.

'Why don't we teach Rocky some tricks, so we can surprise Dad when he gets home?' suggested Darren. 'Then he might not be so bothered that Rocky can't run.'

'I'm not sure Rocky's ready to learn anything new yet,' I replied.

'Zack's dog can do sit and beg, and lets you shake his paw,' Darren went on. 'Think how pleased Dad would be if Rocky could do that.'

'OK then, we can give it a try,' I agreed.

Darren stood in front of Rocky. 'SIT, Rocky, SIT!' he shouted loudly.

Rocky just looked up at him, as if to ask what on earth he was talking about.

'SIT, Rocky, SIT!' Darren repeated, even louder.

This time, Rocky yawned and walked off.

'Here, let me try – you're not doing it right.' I told him. I'd seen a programme on the television about training dogs and they made it look easy. I stared Rocky straight in the eyes and pointed my finger at him. 'Siiii –ITT, Rocky! Siiii –ITT, Rocky!' I commanded, making my voice go up high at the end, like the dog trainer on TV.

Rocky lay down and shut his eyes.

'Down, Rocky, down! STAY!!' ordered Darren quickly. 'He can do that all right, can't he?'

'Well done, Darren,' I said, sarcastically, 'now why don't you try telling him to get up?'

'What're you lot doing with that dog now?' came a familiar voice. Old Wilf was back on his chair, watching us over the fence.

'We're teaching him some tricks,' Darren told him.

'Tricks? Tricks?' Wilf repeated. 'You don't teach a greyhound tricks! He's a racing dog, not a circus performer!'

'We were only getting him to sit,' said Darren sulkily.

'How long've you lot had that animal now?' asked Wilf.

'Eight weeks,' I replied.

'And haven't you learned nothing about greyhounds yet?' sighed Old Wilf.

'Actually, we've been reading library books and looking up lots of information on the computer – especially Darren,' I answered back.

'Computers! Don't talk to me about computers! Waste of time! How're you going to learn about dogs from some machine?' grumbled Wilf. 'All you gotta do is look at the shape of him. See the size of those back legs? He can't sit proper with legs that big, so why're you telling him to do it?'

I felt a bit stupid, because when you looked at Rocky it was obvious Wilf was right.

'My friend Zack's dog does all sort of tricks,' said Darren.

'Then if you'd wanted a daft dog you should've got one,' Wilf snapped back. 'A greyhound's built to run and that's the end of it.'

'But we told you Rocky's broken his leg – he can't run.' I was fed up with Old Wilf keep telling us we were doing everything wrong.

'Nothing wrong with that dog, except he's been knocked about a bit,' argued Wilf. 'Lost his confidence, that's all. Needs you to help him along.'

In spite of all his grumbling, Wilf did seem to know what he was talking about. I began to wonder if he might be able to help us.

'What do you think we should do?' I asked him.

'Yeah, have you got any good ideas?' asked Darren.

At first, Wilf looked as if he thought we were messing him about: I don't think he could believe we were really asking for his advice. But he must have realised we were serious, because he stopped sounding cross for once.

'Start by remembering the kind of dog he is – work with his nature,' he said, almost kindly.

We both looked puzzled.

'All right then,' Wilf continued, 'you tell me you've been finding out about greyhounds. What sort of dogs are they?'

'That's easy – they're hunting dogs,' said Darren, showing off.

'Good,' said Wilf, 'that means they're built to chase things what move, especially if they're small and furry. That's what they're born to do and your Rocky won't have forgotten it. When he saw that rabbit at the vet's, what happened?'

'He just went for it,' I said.

'And when he thought your Gran was wearing a rabbit?'

'He jumped the fence.'

'Told you so!' repeated Old Wilf excitedly. 'Couldn't help himself, could he? Didn't think about his bad leg then!'

'But we haven't got a rabbit for Rocky to chase,' put in Darren.

Wilf sighed, 'I know that, don't I? You've got to

find something else for him to run after. He won't want to run unless he's got something to chase. When we raced the whippets in the old days, we shook a rag at them.'

'Will this do?' I asked, picking up Dad's old T-shirt – the one that went everywhere with Rocky.

'That's just the thing! And he needs a reward – for when he gets to it.'

'He's eaten all the pigs' ears,' I said.

'Try him with these.' Wilf reached into his pocket and handed Darren a packet of multi-coloured dog treats. Rocky stood up with his ears pricked the moment he smelt them. 'My Molly used to love them.'

'Your wife loved dog chews?' asked Darren in amazement.

'Are you daft or something?' said Wilf indignantly. 'Molly was me whippet, not me missus!'

'Did you go and buy these specially for Rocky, Wilf?' I asked him.

'Nothing special about it – just happened to be passing the pet shop when I went for me paper.'

'They're wicked!' said Darren. 'Thanks, Wilf!'

Wilf had a sudden coughing fit, so he couldn't reply.

'Right, then, let's get going,' he said, when he'd got his breath back. 'Anna, you hold his collar, and Darren – you grab that T-shirt and stand a few steps away.'

We did as we were told, but it was a real surprise to find out Wilf knew our names. We'd only ever heard him shout 'Oi, you!' at us before.

'Now, Darren,' Wilf carried on, when we were in the right position, 'shake that thing for all you're worth. And call him.'

Darren did as he was told. Rocky looked over, but he didn't move.

'Go on, lad,' encouraged Old Wilf, 'a bit louder this time – he can do it!'

'Come on, Rocky! Come on, Rocky!' Darren shouted, waving the T-shirt in front of him.

Nothing happened at first. Then, all of a sudden, Rocky's head went up. I felt him pull on his collar and I let go. Off he walked over to where Darren was standing!

'Praise him up and give him a treat!' called Wilf. 'Now bring him back, Anna, and stand a bit further away, Darren.'

Step by step, we got Rocky to move further each time, but he was still only walking.

'Right,' said Wilf, 'now he's got the idea, he needs some more room. Take him right down the front path, Anna, and Darren, stand as far back as you can.'

We got in position, then Darren began to wave and call again.

Rocky started to walk forward but, suddenly, after

a few strides, he began to get faster. The next moment, all four of his legs were moving strongly, picking up speed till he was trotting along, back to where Darren was waiting.

Darren and I began to jump up and down, while Old Wilf bounced so hard on his chair I thought he was going to fall off. I hugged Rocky and then Darren hugged Rocky and we gave him a whole handful of dog treats. Rocky wagged his tail, round and round like he always did when he was pleased, while we made a great fuss of him.

'I told you! I told you!' Old Wilf yelled. 'Nothing wrong with that dog! He's not running yet, but he soon will be!'

CHAPTER 27

'Isn't it great, Anna, what Rocky can do?' Darren was so excited. 'Just wait till we tell Dad!'

'No! We mustn't say anything! Not yet!' I jumped on him.

I'd suddenly had an idea – the one I'd been waiting for. The big idea that would keep us all in my special family picture.

'We're going to practise until Rocky can really run again and then show everyone,' I explained. 'It's Dad's birthday soon. Let's surprise Dad on his birthday.'

'Like a special present?' asked Darren.

'Exactly,' I replied.

'You both have to promise not to tell anybody,' I went on.

'My lips are sealed,' said Wilf.

'What, nobody at all?' Darren asked. 'Not even Marcus? Marcus can keep a secret.'

'And how do you know that?' I was fed up with

hearing about Marcus.

'At school, he never told Mr Ahmed that it was me put superglue on his chair, even though he got detention for it.'

I bet Mum didn't know about that! But I knew how much Marcus loved Rocky and how Rocky trusted him. And I remembered Marcus telling Dad to give Rocky a chance, like perhaps he wanted a chance himself.

'All right, then,' I said. 'You can tell Marcus, but absolutely, positively, nobody else.'

Wilf started to climb down off his chair. 'I'll leave you to it, then. Can see you don't need me anymore.'

'Wait!' I shouted. 'You've got to help us. We need you to make sure we do it right.'

Wilf paused. 'What, me? Help you? With the dog?' he said finally. 'Well, all right, then,' and he got down with a big smile on his face.

There weren't many times when we could practise, as we had to wait till Mum and Dad were both out, but Rocky loved every moment. He looked like he was finding out what he was made for, all over again. And he nearly gave the game away. Whenever he saw Darren, Marcus and me together, he'd get up and stand by the back door, wagging his tail.

'What's Rocky after?' asked Dad, the first time it happened.

'He's waiting to …' Darren managed to stop in

time.

'Waiting to do what?' asked Dad.

'To have a walk round the garden,' was all I could think of. It was pretty feeble, but Dad looked convinced.

It was a lot harder trying to keep things from Mum. Once, she caught us with the calendar, trying to work out when we next had the house to ourselves.

'What are you up to?' she asked straight away.

'Nothing,' replied Darren, trying to look all innocent.

'I know something's going on – the way you keep whispering together,' she went on.

'It's a surprise,' I tried, 'we're planning a surprise present for Dad's birthday.'

'That's right, and it's a secret,' Darren backed me up.

'But it's a nice secret,' I tried to reassure her. 'We just don't want anyone to know yet.'

Mum still looked suspicious. 'All right, then,' she said at last, 'but if I find out it's one of Darren's practical jokes, there'll be trouble!'

Later that evening, when I was doing my homework, Mum came into my room.

'I've been having a think, about what you said about a surprise for Dad's birthday,' she said, sitting down on the bed.

'I can't tell you what it is, Mum,' I told her.

'No, love, I didn't mean that. It's just that I thought, perhaps I could plan something too. Make it a bit special.'

'Really? Are you sure?' I asked, amazed she'd suggested it.

Mum had always said she'd never, ever do anything for Dad's birthday again, after what happened three years ago. She'd spent ages organising this party, and got in loads of food and drink. Only Dad forgot all about it and didn't come home till after midnight, dead drunk, from the pub. Since then, Dad's birthdays just seemed to bring back terrible memories of the row that had gone on for weeks.

'I could make a cake and do us a nice tea – nothing too fancy, mind,' Mum carried on.

'It's a great idea!' I was so pleased.

'And we could invite Marcus and your Gran – if I get another bottle of gin, and perhaps Old Wilf might come; he's always talking to your Dad lately.'

'And Rocky! Can Rocky come too, Mum? Please say yes!' I begged.

'Of course he can, love. We couldn't manage without Rocky,' she laughed.

'So it'll be like a real family celebration, won't it?' I gave her a hug.

'Yes, it will, Anna. And we haven't had one of those in a long time,' Mum replied.

145

CHAPTER 28

The next Tuesday, I couldn't wait for school to finish. We'd done all the training we could do at home and now we were taking Rocky to the park for his first run. I felt certain that this was going to be the big day.

I made a dash for the gate as soon as the bell went.

'Aren't you walking home with us?' called Alisha.

'Sorry, can't stop … see you tomorrow,' was all I had time to say.

Darren and Marcus were ahead of me and I had to run to catch them up. We reached the end of our street in world-record time, but I knew something wasn't right.

'Listen!' I told the boys. 'Can you hear that?'

'Hear what?' asked Darren. 'I can't hear …'

'Shut up for a minute and listen,' I said.

There was no mistaking that noise. Close by, a dog

was howling. And not just any dog.

'It's Rocky!' Darren said at once.

Rocky hadn't made a noise like that since the first night Dad brought him home.

'Perhaps he's hurt ...' I began, but Darren and Marcus were already running down the street and I had to chase after them.

We ran straight into the garden. Rocky was pacing up and down by the fence, yowling and barking. Darren grabbed hold of him and tried to keep him still, but Rocky kept struggling to get away. So Marcus picked up Dad's old T-shirt and wrapped it round Rocky and held on to him tightly.

'Is he all right?' I asked.

Rocky was quieter now, but his eyes were wide and staring and he was trembling.

'He's OK, just frightened,' said Marcus.

'But what's got into him?' I wondered. There was no sign of anything in the garden that could have upset Rocky so much. 'Let's take him indoors till he's calmed down.'

Marcus and Darren tried to lead Rocky into the house, but he wouldn't move. He kept pulling them back towards the fence.

It was Darren who thought of what to do next. 'Come on, Marcus, help me carry the bench,' he said.

I grabbed Rocky, while the boys dragged our

147

garden bench over to the fence and jumped up on it. Darren let out a yell when he saw what was on the other side.

'It's Wilf! Quick, Anna! Come and look!' he shrieked.

I let go of Rocky and scrambled onto the bench. Wilf was lying stretched out on the ground, his one leg at a funny angle. There was a small pool of blood on the path by his head. His eyes were closed and he wasn't moving. I felt my legs go all wobbly and thought for a minute I was going to be sick.

'He's dead! He's dead! Wilf's dead!' Darren shouted.

I took a deep breath to try and pull myself together. 'Shut up, Darren! Go and get my mobile,' I ordered.

Darren leaped down, grabbed my school bag and tipped everything out, scattering books and pens over the lawn.

'Hurry up, will you?' I yelled at him.

At the same time, Marcus clambered over the top of the fence and lowered himself onto the other side. He knelt down beside Wilf and put his cheek close to his mouth. Then he very gently felt Wilf's wrist and the side of his neck.

'He ain't dead. He's breathing and he's got a pulse,' called Marcus.

Darren came racing back with my mobile. 'Call Mum, Anna – she'll know what to do!' he begged.

'Ambulance first!' Marcus snapped back. 'Dial 999! Do it!'

I made the call. 'Come on, come on!' I muttered, as I heard it ringing.

'Wake him up, Marcus!' Darren shouted. 'Help him sit up!'

'No, mustn't move him. Bring us something to keep him warm,' Marcus replied.

Darren ran off to fetch a blanket.

At last someone answered. 'They're asking me all sorts of questions!' I called.

'Give it 'ere,' snapped Marcus, reaching up and grabbing the phone.

I heard the words 'airway' and 'heart rate' and something called 'CPR', which I'd only ever come across on that TV hospital programme. And that's when I started to notice things: Wilf's chair was lying on its side, with one leg snapped off and there were dog chews scattered over the ground. I thought I could guess what had happened.

'Ambulance is coming, the police as well,' Marcus reported.

'Where's Rocky?' asked Darren, when things went quiet for a moment.

I'd forgotten all about Rocky and how upset he'd been. At first, we couldn't see where he'd got to, then I found him under the bench.

'Rocky's fine, he's fast asleep,' I said. Then I rang

Mum at the supermarket.

'Mum,' I said, when she answered, 'can you come home quick? There's been an accident.' I heard her gasp. 'No, we're all right – it's Old Wilf; he's hurt himself and it looks really bad.'

CHAPTER 29

We heard the siren coming down the street and Marcus ran into Wilf's house to let the ambulance men in. They got to work on Wilf immediately, putting in tubes and examining him all over. Soon after, a police car pulled up and suddenly Wilf's garden was full of men in uniform. The officer made straight for Marcus.

'Well, if it isn't Marcus Harding,' he said. 'Always knew I'd run into you again. What've you been up to this time?'

Marcus glowered at the policeman and mumbled something.

'Mind your mouth, lad,' snapped the officer, 'or you'll be coming with me.'

'But he's with us; he hasn't done anything!' I shouted.

Then I heard footsteps running down the side path.

'Anna! Darren! What's happened?' It was Mum.

'Quick, Mum!' yelled Darren, trying not to cry. 'Wilf's hurt and Marcus is in trouble!'

Mum climbed on the bench beside us. I suppose we must have looked a bit stupid: the three of us standing there like that, but it didn't seem to matter at the time.

'What's going on, officer?' she called. 'I'm Jo Stephenson; I live here.'

'PC Alan Canning,' the officer introduced himself. 'I've been called to an incident at this house.'

'These are my children, Anna and Darren, and that boy you're holding is their friend,' Mum carried on.

'Some friend they've got, Mrs Stephenson. We've had dealings with this boy before. I suspect he might have been trying to rob this gentleman.'

'That's not right, Mum!' I interrupted.

'Marcus wouldn't do anything like that,' Mum said sternly.

Meanwhile, the paramedics had got Wilf onto a stretcher. 'Hang on a second,' the older one said, 'this lad hasn't done anything wrong. He's the one who let us in and he's been looking after the old man.' Then they hurried out to the ambulance.

PC Canning still didn't look convinced.

'But I know what happened!' I tried to explain.

'I think you'd better listen to my daughter,' Mum said.

'All right then, young lady,' the police officer turned to me, 'tell me exactly what's been going on here.'

I explained how we'd run home when we heard Rocky barking and how we'd found Wilf and how Marcus had helped him. Rocky must have heard his name, because he woke up and came to see what was going on. He scrambled up on the bench as well, and put his front paws on the fence to get a better look. Now there were four of us standing up there.

'That doesn't tell us how the gentleman got hurt,' said PC Canning.

'Wilf's always looking over our fence,' I went on. 'He stands on that chair so he can see. And he loves Rocky, our greyhound. Wilf likes to give him a treat. He must have been reaching over, when the chair broke and he fell and injured himself. It was an accident!'

The policeman had a good look round. He saw the broken chair, the spilt dog chews and Rocky's face over the fence. He didn't say anything at first. Then, finally, he stepped away from Marcus.

'Very well,' he said, 'I'll just come and take down a few details – if that's all right with you, Mrs Stephenson.

At last we could get down off the bench. We all went into the kitchen and Mum made tea for everyone. Rocky stood close to Marcus all the time, like he was making sure no one took his friend away while he was around.

I had to repeat everything that had happened, while PC Canning made notes. Then he had a few final questions.

'What's the old gentleman's full name?' he asked.

'Wilf,' replied Mum, 'we only know him as Wilf.'

'Any family? Friends?'

'None that I know of; he never has any visitors.'

'In that case, I'll have to notify Social Services. Meanwhile, I'll make sure the house is secure. Thank you very much, Mrs Stephenson, children.' PC Canning stood up and gave Marcus a last look before he left. He seemed almost sorry he wasn't taking him to the police station.

Mum went to see the officer out. We heard her give him a good telling off. I caught the words, '… be more careful who you blame … Marcus is a good boy …' After Mum had finished with him, I didn't think he'd be jumping to conclusions quite so quickly in future.

A minute later, I heard the front door being flung open. Rocky's ears went up and his tail started to go round and round, so it was no surprise to see Dad come bursting in.

'Is everything all right, Jo?' he said.

'Dad!' shouted Darren, 'Wilf's nearly dead and Rocky found him and a policeman wanted to arrest Marcus …'

'Hang on a minute, son. Let's take it a bit at a time,' said Dad.

'There's no need to worry, Pete,' Mum reassured him, 'and Darren – you'd better let Anna tell your Dad the story.'

So I had to go over everything yet again, while Rocky did a little dance round Dad's legs till he got himself noticed.

'I don't know what would have happened to Wilf, if the children hadn't found him,' said Mum. 'They were brilliant – especially you, Marcus. However did you know what to do?'

Marcus didn't reply at first, then he muttered, 'It's 'cos of me mum. Had to sort her out. Lots of times.'

That was something none of us knew about. I looked at Marcus as if I was seeing him properly for the first time.

'But it was all down to Rocky really,' I said. 'He knew Wilf was in trouble'.

'Saved his life,' said Marcus.

'Well done, old boy, well done,' said Dad. 'Looks like we'll have to change your name to Superdog!'

Rocky looked as if he didn't mind what he was called – just as long as he kept getting this much attention.

CHAPTER 30

'How's Wilf?' I asked Mum as soon as I got home next day. I knew she'd been to the hospital to see him.

'Not too good, love,' Mum replied. 'His leg's broken and that can be very serious at his age. Wilf's eighty-six, would you believe? And he hit his head badly when he fell. He's got concussion and it's made him very confused.'

'Poor Wilf!' I said. 'It sounds terrible.'

'But it could have been much worse. The doctors reckon he'd been lying there for ages and he might have died if you hadn't found him.'

'Will he be out of hospital this week? I asked.

'I shouldn't think so!'

'What about next week?'

'It's not very likely.' Mum replied.

This didn't look good. I was worried about Wilf, of course, but now it didn't look like he'd be able to come to the park with Rocky. We'd missed our big practice and time was running out.

When Marcus came round, I got him and Darren to meet me in the shed. We had to make some emergency plans.

'Wilf's got to stay in hospital, so we need to carry on without him,' I told them.

'Carry on with what?' asked Darren.

'Down the park? Rocky? Run? Remember?' I said.

Even Marcus was quicker than my brother. 'Yeah, right. We knows what to do, Wilf showed us.'

'So, after school on Monday, Mum's working late and Dad won't get back till six. That's when we do it,' I told them. 'All agreed?'

When the day came, Darren and Marcus were already waiting by the front door for me. Rocky looked really excited. He was eager for his walk and started pulling on the lead the nearer we got to the park. I felt more and more confident with every step: Rocky was going to run, at last!

When we arrived, we made for the big, open ground in the centre. Rocky looked all set, as if he couldn't wait to get going.

I got everyone sorted out. 'Marcus: you have the dog treats, Darren: you wave the T-shirt. I'll hold Rocky.'

'That's not fair, why can't I hold Rocky?' Darren

started.

'Stop arguing and do it.' I wasn't about to waste any time.

I walked Rocky about twenty metres away from the boys, took off his lead and held him by the collar.

'OK, Darren,' I shouted, 'call him – just like you did in the garden.'

Darren began waving and shouting and I waited for the tug on the collar that would tell me Rocky was ready to go. Nothing happened.

'Come on, Darren!' I yelled. 'You're being useless! Call him properly.'

Darren waved and shouted some more. Rocky looked up at me, but he didn't move.

'I told you I should've held him,' Darren came storming across. 'Give him to me – you're not doing it right.'

We changed places. This time Rocky walked slowly over to where I was waiting and gobbled up his treat. That was a good start, but no matter how many times we tried, he wouldn't do it a second time.

'Give us a try with him,' said Marcus.

Rocky walked all round Marcus and wagged his tail, like he thought this was a good game. He didn't even look at me and Darren.

'I think he needs a bigger space,' I suggested.

So we tried standing further apart. Then we tried standing closer together. We kept changing places.

We tried bribing him with three dog treats at once. It didn't matter what we did, Rocky wasn't the least bit interested.

I could feel this great wave of anger washing all over me. I walked up to Rocky and, 'Come on, you stupid dog! Move, will you!' I shouted.

'Shut up, Anna! Don't you talk to him like that!' Darren shouted back.

Then we carried on yelling and screaming at each other till Marcus stepped between us.

'Back off, will you? You're scaring him,' he said.

Rocky had shuffled closer to Marcus. His head was down and he was trembling. Worst of all, he was even holding his bad leg off the ground again.

'Now look what you've done!' Darren shrieked at me.

Hot tears began to sting my eyes and I rubbed them away with my fists. 'I wouldn't have done it, if he'd run like he was supposed to,' I shouted.

'You and your stupid, big ideas!' Darren kept on.

'Shut it, both of you!' snapped Marcus.

'Don't know why Rocky has to run, anyway,' Darren had to have the last word, although he said it quietly. 'Come on, Marcus, we're taking Rocky home before she frightens him any more.'

'You don't understand, do you?' I yelled.

But they'd already marched off, leaving me to walk back on my own.

When I got in, I went straight up to my bedroom and stayed there. I felt so bad about upsetting Rocky I couldn't face seeing anyone. I said I had a headache when Mum came to see what was the matter. Then Dad made me some hot chocolate and that just started me crying.

I couldn't get to sleep that night, so, when I was sure everyone was in bed, I crept down to the kitchen. Rocky slept there sometimes now and he was lying in his favourite spot under the table.

'Sorry, Rocky, sorry I was horrible to you,' I whispered, stroking his side. 'I was desperate for you to run, so I could show Dad. His job's going to end soon and I'm scared he'll start having more of his big ideas. I wanted to prove to him that if you stick with things, they come right in the end. But they don't always, I know, and it's not your fault.'

Rocky made those snuffling sounds he does when he's asleep. I hoped it was his way of saying he'd forgiven me.

CHAPTER 31

The next morning, I got up early and dashed down to the kitchen. I was desperate to find out if Rocky was all right. I can't tell you how relieved I was to see him looking his usual lively self and walking around without any signs of a limp.

Even so, it was hard having my plans fall apart. I'd built up so many hopes about Rocky running again and what it would mean to Dad, I couldn't get over the disappointment that they'd all come to nothing. I felt like I had a great big weight tied to each foot, which I was dragging along everywhere.

Mum was concerned. 'You look a bit under the weather, love. Do you need the day off school?' she asked.

But I didn't want to stop at home: there'd be nothing to take my mind off feeling miserable. It didn't help that Darren was ignoring me. I tried to make it up with him loads of times, but he always walked away.

'I can see you two have been arguing again,' Mum said that evening, when we were washing up. 'Is that why you're upset?'

'Me? Upset about Darren? I don't think so!' I answered back.

'Is it anything to do with this special present for Dad's birthday?' she asked.

Why does Mum always know what's going on? I really did want to tell her everything, but I'd made a promise to keep it secret. Instead, I flung the tea towel down. 'Nothing's the matter,' I snapped, 'and there isn't going to be a surprise any more.'

'But I thought you were planning …' Mum wouldn't give up.

'Well, I've changed my mind. Now, leave me alone and stop going on about it!' I shouted.

Dad walked in and saw the look on both our faces. 'Oh no, not women's troubles!' he joked. 'Don't tell me I've got to put up with two moody women in the house now!'

'Shut up, Pete,' said Mum, 'we're having a chat, that's all.'

'Think I'd better take Rocky for his walk, then; us men know when we're not wanted.' Dad whistled cheerfully for Rocky and put on his lead, giving me the chance to escape up to my bedroom.

At least Rocky wasn't sulking and still looked pleased to see me. The next day, I was giving him an extra-special grooming in the garden when Marcus called round. He went into the house and came straight back out, pulling Darren along with him.

'Here, you two – get over it!' Marcus ordered, shoving Darren towards me.

'It was her fault! I didn't start it! It wasn't me what shouted at Rocky, or scared him, or …' Darren went on and on.

Marcus waited till he'd run out of steam. 'Look at the dog. He's the one what got shouted at. He's all right, ain't he? I said, ain't he?' Marcus repeated, until Darren finally nodded his head.

'I've been trying to tell you I was sorry, but you wouldn't listen,' I said to Darren.

'D'yer hear that?' asked Marcus.

'Yeah, well …' mumbled Darren.

'Dog's got over it, so you get over it,' Marcus told him.

Darren shrugged his shoulders as if he didn't care, but I knew what Marcus thought mattered to him more than anything. 'If Rocky's not bothered, then I suppose it's all right,' he said eventually. That was better than you usually got from my brother.

The boys walked off, then they paused to talk about something and came back.

'Tell her what you said, Darren,' Marcus gave him another push.

'I said, you mustn't mind so much, Anna, about

Rocky not running, I mean. Dad loves him anyway,' Darren mumbled. Then they both walked away before I had time to answer.

Maybe I'd got it wrong. Perhaps Rocky's best chance was for me to accept him how he was and still love him, like Dad did. I knew I could live with that and, like magic, I felt those weights at the end of my legs begin to get lighter.

So, what if Rocky was the only greyhound in the world who couldn't run? It really didn't matter – did it?

CHAPTER 32

Either Mum or Dad went to visit Wilf every day.
Mum said they were the only visitors he ever had.
A week went by before we heard any good news: at
last Wilf was on the mend.

'The doctors say he's made a remarkable recovery,'
Mum told us, when she got back from the hospital.
'His head's still sore and his leg's in plaster, but he got
out of bed today and he's sitting up.'

'He must be as tough as old boots,' said Dad.

'He doesn't seem like the same Old Wilf, though,'
Mum went on. 'The fall's left him very shaky and he
hates having to depend on other people.'

'Will he be coming home soon?' asked Darren.

'No, not yet: they don't think he's ready to look
after himself properly. The social worker's found him
somewhere to stay,' Mum explained.

'Wilf and Social Services?' laughed Dad. 'I can
imagine how well they get on together!'

'He's moving into *The Willows* tomorrow – you know, the place on the other side of the park,' said Mum.

'Wilf in an old people's home?' said Dad. 'Are they trying to finish him off?'

'That's enough, Pete,' Mum told him, 'and it's called a *Residential Care Home*, actually.'

'Same thing,' muttered Dad.

'Then can we visit him?' I asked

'I'm sure you can,' agreed Mum.

We arranged that Dad would take me on Saturday, when Wilf had had a few days to settle in. Darren wanted to go as well, but Mum thought too many visitors at once wasn't a good idea.

As the home was nearby, Dad and I decided to walk there. We went down to the park, where we take Rocky, then walked all the way through to the small entrance at the far end. The Willows was on the opposite side of the road, hidden behind a tall hedge.

'They certainly don't want anyone escaping from here,' joked Dad, as he pushed open a heavy gate.

We walked up a gravelled drive to the front porch of a big, old house, with two enormous bay windows on each floor. Dad rang the bell and we heard it echoing inside.

'Yes? Can I help you?' asked the lady who opened the door. She had short, grey hair and was smartly dressed in a dark blue suit. It didn't look like she smiled very often.

'Hello,' said Dad, 'we're Pete and Anna Stephenson and we've come to see Wilf.'

'Wilf?' repeated the woman.

'That's right; he was moved here on Wednesday.'

'Do you mean Mr Willetts?' she asked.

'Yes, Mr Willetts,' said Dad. 'Sorry, but we always call him Wilf.'

'I'm Mrs Appleby, the matron. Come in, please.'

Mrs Appleby led us into an oak-panelled hall, with a desk in one corner. 'You'll need to sign the visitors' book.' She handed Dad a pen. 'Are you family?'

'No, we're next-door neighbours; Wilf doesn't have any family,' replied Dad.

'Most of our residents are in the lounge, if you'll follow me. And we do require that children are kept under strict control at all times.' Mrs Appleby gave me a withering look.

'Do you hear that, Anna?' said Dad, with a wink. 'Absolutely no rampaging around while you're here!'

Mrs Appleby set off at a cracking pace, so that Dad and I nearly had to run to keep up with her. We went down a long corridor, with doors on either side. Everywhere was spotlessly clean and polished, but there was a faint smell in the background you couldn't get away from. It was like a mixture of bleach and something else I didn't want to think about.

167

Mrs Appleby showed us into a big room at the back of the house. There were chairs arranged all round the edge, each one occupied by an elderly man or woman. A television was playing loudly in one corner. Only two or three people were watching the screen, while the others were either asleep or staring into space. There was no sign of Wilf.

'Mr Willetts must be on the terrace,' explained Mrs Appleby, stifling a sigh. 'He likes to sit outside. You'll find him through there.' She pointed to a glass door and walked off.

The 'terrace' turned out to be a small area of cracked concrete surrounded by a high wall, where the dustbins were kept. Hunched up in a wheelchair, with one leg propped up on a stool, was a little old man wearing a dressing gown. He was dozing with his head on one side and his mouth open.

'Hello there, Wilf!' called Dad cheerfully.

For a moment, I was completely taken aback. I couldn't believe this was Wilf!

'Eh? What? Who's there?' he said, waking up with a start.

'It's Pete. Look, I've brought Anna to see you,' Dad replied.

'Hello, Wilf!' I tried to sound as cheerful as I could. Close up, Wilf looked all clean and polished too. Someone had even combed his hair into a side parting.

'What are you doing out here, when you've got that nice room to sit in?' Dad asked.

'Only place they'll let me have a smoke,' grumbled Wilf, but at least it sounded more like him. 'And you've seen that lot in there. The living dead, that's what they are. Rather be out here on my own than with that bunch of …'

'Like a four-star hotel, this is,' interrupted Dad. 'Three meals a day and people to look after you.'

'Always looked after meself,' snarled Wilf, 'till some young whipper-snapper decides I needs looking after! I told that social work girl, I didn't fight all through the War for people like you to tell me what I needs.'

'Still, it's not for long, just till you get on your feet again. You'll be back home in no time,' said Dad brightly.

That only seemed to make things worse. 'Nobody comes out of these places,' mumbled Wilf, 'except when they're carried out in a box.'

It was awful hearing Wilf talking like that, about dying and everything. I tried to change the subject. 'Darren and Marcus send their love and Rocky misses you loads.'

'Rocky? Rocky?' Wilf perked up for the first time. 'How's that Rocky doing?' Then he turned to Dad, 'Think I've left me matches somewhere. Go and find them for us, will you Pete?'

Wilf waited till Dad had gone in, then looked at me excitedly, 'Has Rocky run, yet? Has he? Like we planned?'

I couldn't bring myself to tell him what had really happened. 'Everything's fine, Wilf, just like you said it'd be.'

'Told you so! Told you that dog could run! And wait till your Dad finds out! What day is it today?'

'Saturday,' I told him.

'Then it'll be Pete's birthday on Monday – there, I haven't forgotten everything, not yet. Wish I could be there to see the look on everybody's face when old Rocky ...' Wilf's voice faded away. He gave a big sigh and slumped down in his wheelchair.

Dad came back. 'Can't see your matches anywhere, Wilf. Try your pockets again.'

But Wilf's eyes were closing. 'Come on, Molly,' he mumbled, 'time for your walk. Come on, girl ...'

'Who's Molly?' whispered Dad.

'Wilf's whippet – from ages ago, when he was a young man,' I replied.

Dad shook his head sadly, then we both crept away, leaving Wilf to dream about better days.

CHAPTER 33

'All the spark had gone out of him,' I heard Dad telling Mum about Wilf. 'And he was rambling on about some dog he used to have. Putting him in that home was the worst thing that could have happened. It's like he's given up.'

'Still, I expect he was pleased to see Anna,' said Mum.

'He wasn't bothered and he never even asked about the boys. The way Wilf feels now, I think he wishes they'd never found him,' Dad replied.

'Don't say that, Pete!' Mum sounded alarmed. 'I'll go along tomorrow and see what I can do.'

But when Mum came back from The Willows on Sunday, she was even more concerned. 'He wouldn't see me,' she told us. 'That stuck-up Mrs Apple-Pie woman said Wilf didn't want visitors and she wouldn't even let me in.'

We were all worried about Wilf, but we had other

important things to think about. Monday was Dad's big day and Mum said nothing was getting in the way of us having a good time.

When I got home from school, Mum had put balloons over the front door and Darren was making a poster for the window, which said: *'HAPY BITHDAY PETE'*. The house was filled with the smell of cooking and there was a cake ready for icing. I was surprised to see Rocky licking out the mixing bowl. He was pushing it all around the kitchen floor as he tried to get at every last bit.

'Just this once, Anna,' said Mum, 'it's a special occasion for Rocky as well.'

Two saucepans were bubbling on the cooker. 'I've made your Dad's favourite: chicken curry. One pan's for us; the other's super-duper, fiery-furnace hot – how your Dad likes it,' Mum explained. 'I've only got the rice to do, so that can wait till everyone's here. Dad's leaving work early and Marcus and Gran are coming at six o'clock.'

I went upstairs to fetch my present and put it with the others. I'd bought Dad a key ring and pin badge from the Retired Greyhound Trust, which Mum had helped me order on-line. Dad wouldn't get his other present, seeing Rocky run, but I didn't feel so bad about that any more. Still, just thinking about it reminded me of other things.

'Something bothering you, love?' asked Mum, as I

was laying the table.

'I was just wondering what was going to happen later on – when Dad finishes that job at the building site.'

'I don't know, love,' said Mum, 'we'll have to wait and see. Perhaps there'll be something else he can do.'

'But aren't you worried? What if things go back to how they used to be?' I asked.

Mum stopped what she was doing and put her arms round me. 'Everything's fine right now and that's what matters,' she told me. 'And if things do change, we'll still have these good times to hold on to – they won't go away.'

Suddenly the doorbell rang. Somebody was keeping their finger on the button because it didn't stop. Then, whoever it was started banging on the door as well.

'Go and see who's making that racket, please, Anna,' grumbled Mum.

It was Marcus. 'Why are you here so early?' I asked.

Marcus couldn't speak. He was bent over trying to get his breath, as if he'd run all the way. 'Wilf weren't there,' he spluttered eventually.

'What are you on about?' I said. I had no idea.

'Wilf weren't there,' he said again, then he grabbed me by the arm and pulled me into the garden.

'Get off, Marcus!' I yelled at him.

173

'Listen,' he said, when he could talk properly, 'that day we tried to run Rocky – Wilf weren't there!'

'I know that, stupid! He was in hospital.'

'Stupid yourself!' Marcus snapped back. 'You ain't listening! The dog sees Wilf – he knows he's gotta run. But Wilf weren't there – in the park.'

A light switched on in my head. 'You mean, every single time we were training Rocky, Wilf was there, so Rocky wouldn't run that day because Wilf was missing?' I said.

'Yeah,' said Marcus.

'So if Wilf came to the park today, Rocky would run and Dad could still get his birthday surprise?'

'Yeah,' said Marcus.

It was so simple, I couldn't believe I hadn't thought of it myself. 'Marcus, has anyone ever told you you're absolutely brilliant?' I said.

'No,' said Marcus, his face turning even redder.

I knew what we had to do. 'Go and get Darren and I'll fetch Rocky,' I ordered him.

'We're going to run Rocky in the park, to show Dad, just like we planned,' I told Darren, when I'd finishing explaining Marcus's brainwave.

'But we need Wilf,' objected Darren, 'and Wilf's in The Willows! And he's got his leg in plaster. And he won't see anybody. How's he going to come to the park?'

'Me and Marcus are going to fetch him, aren't we,

174

Marcus?' I said, as confidently as I could. I had no idea how we were going to do it, but I knew nothing was going to stop me. Marcus looked doubtful, although he nodded all the same. 'We're taking Rocky with us. Your job is to bring Mum, Dad and Gran down to the other end of park at the same time. But DON'T tell them what's going on.'

'How am I supposed to do that?' gasped Darren.

'Think of something – think of anything. And when you get them there, this is what I want you to do …'

CHAPTER 34

Marcus and I set off for The Willows, leaving Darren behind to deal with Mum. Rocky loped along beside us, his tail wagging. He seemed to sense that something was going on and he was excited to be part of it.

I stopped when we got to the gate. The Willows looked so big and forbidding, with those huge windows staring at me like giant eyes. Getting Wilf out of there seemed impossible and I wondered where I'd got such a daft idea from in the first place.

Marcus saw me hesitate. 'Get on with it,' he said, opening the gate and marching up to the main entrance with Rocky, so I had to follow him.

Mrs Appleby answered the door. She looked Marcus, Rocky and me up and down. 'Can I help you?' she asked, in a way that meant she certainly didn't want to.

'I'm Anna Stephenson, I've been here before, with

my father.' My voice started off all shaky, but it got stronger the longer I carried on. 'Please can we see Wilf, I mean Mr Willetts?'

Mrs Appleby stared at me as if I'd been sick over the porch. 'Mr Willetts isn't receiving visitors at the moment,' she replied and started to close the door.

'Wait a minute, please!' I called. 'Wilf loves our dog, Rocky, and if we could take him in and show him …'

'Certainly not!' Mrs Appleby was indignant. 'I don't permit any animals in the home, especially dogs. And neither of you children should be here without an adult.'

She slammed the door in my face. I spent a few minutes ringing the bell again, but no one answered. It wasn't fair! Everything was going wrong again and there was nothing I could do. I fought back the tears welling up in my eyes, while I muttered every bad word I knew.

'I'll have to text Darren and let him know the plan's off,' I turned to Marcus. But Marcus and Rocky had gone. 'Marcus! Marcus!' I called, getting more and more panicky.

A minute later, they both reappeared round the side of the building.

'Where have you been?' I yelled. 'And a lot of good you were, just now!'

'Side gate's open,' said Marcus.

'What do you mean?' I asked.

'Side gate's open – we can get in round the back,' repeated Marcus.

I didn't stop to think. 'Come on!' I said, leading the way.

We came out onto the terrace. Wilf was sitting there on his own, as if he hadn't moved since I last saw him. Rocky recognised Wilf straight away. He let out a bark and began to pull on his lead, till Marcus took him over. Then, Rocky jumped up with his front paws on Wilf's lap and gave his face a great lick.

Wilf had been dozing again. 'Get down, Molly, get down,' he mumbled. Then he opened his eyes. 'Rocky? Rocky? Is it really you?' he asked delightedly, giving him a great hug. 'And Anna and Marcus? What are you doing here?'

'We came to ask you something, Wilf,' I replied.

'What day is it?' Wilf asked

'It's Monday,' I told him. I felt my heart sink. If Wilf didn't even know which day it was, how on earth was I going to explain our plan?

'Then it's your Dad's birthday today. Shouldn't you be at home celebrating?'

Wilf remembered! We might still make it work.

'Hurry up,' whispered Marcus, who was busy keeping a lookout.

I blurted it all out. 'Rocky wouldn't run, Wilf, not without you. I let you think he did, but it isn't true. We need you to come with us, to show Dad – please!'

Wilf hesitated. 'You need me? Rocky needs me?' he asked. Then he sat up in his wheelchair as if he'd suddenly grown tall again. 'Bring those crutches, lad, and move that stool from under my leg.'

He started trying to wheel himself back into the lounge.

I had to stop him. 'We can't go that way: Mrs Appleby wouldn't let us in, so we crept round the side. Nobody knows we're here,' I said.

'Then we'd better leave the same way you got in. Marcus, you push me. Quick as you can, son, no time to hang around,' ordered Wilf.

Marcus began to wheel Wilf round the side of the house and down the drive, while I held Rocky and carried the crutches. Wilf's leg, the one in plaster, was sticking straight out in front, so we had a hard job getting him through the gate. Somehow we managed it and, in no time, we'd crossed the road and were heading for the park.

A text from Darren came through on my mobile: 'REDY WEN U R'.

'Faster, Marcus – they're already there!' I called out.

Marcus picked up speed, so that Wilf had to grab hold of the arms of the wheelchair. Rocky thought this was all great fun: he was acting as if it was the best walk he'd ever been on. Then we were through

179

the park entrance and down the slope to the edge of the open space.

My heart was hammering in my chest and I could hardly breathe. I knew there was no going back: from now on it would be all down to Rocky.

CHAPTER 35

I spotted Gran first, at the opposite end of the park, as she was wearing her bright yellow mini-dress and matching boots. Then I picked out Darren, Dad and Mum standing beside her.

'Help me get up, Marcus!' ordered Wilf, grabbing his crutches and struggling out of his wheelchair onto his one good leg. 'Right, Anna – you know what to do.'

I sent Darren a new text, 'GO!' I saw him pull Dad forward and hand him the T-shirt to wave.

'Take the lead off, Anna, and hold him!' said Wilf.

I knelt down by Rocky and put both hands on his collar. I don't think I'd ever wanted anything so much in my life before. 'You can do it, Rocky, please Rocky,' I whispered in his ear, over and over.

Dad began to wave the T-shirt and call, 'Come on, Rocky! Come on, Rocky!' like Darren had told him, but I could hardly hear.

Rocky looked up in Dad's direction. He didn't move.

'That's useless!' grumbled Wilf, 'Tell your Dad to put a bit of life into it!'

'LOUDER!!!' I sent Darren another message.

Soon I heard Mum, Gran and Darren shouting along with Dad for all they were worth: 'COME ON, ROCKY! COME ON, ROCKY! COME ON!!!'

Rocky's ears pricked up.

'Go on, boy, you can do it!' I urged him, hardly daring to breathe.

That's when I noticed something moving along the ground, just beyond where Dad was standing. I could make out the tip of a bushy tail. It was a squirrel, and Rocky had already seen it. Suddenly, I felt every muscle in his body go tense, like a spring being tightened.

'Let go, Anna!' shouted Wilf.

Rocky pulled so hard, I had no choice. He shot forward. Then he was hurtling over the grass, in great, long-legged bounds. People sometimes say, 'like greased lightening'; well, I've never seen that, but I'm certain Rocky was faster. He crossed the park in a flash, while everyone turned to stare as this blur raced past them.

Dad held out his arms to catch him, but Rocky completely ignored that. He tore past Dad until he'd reached the foot of the tree where the squirrel had escaped to, and started jumping up at the trunk and barking.

It had all happened so quickly, I couldn't take it in at first. I could see Marcus leaping up and down and Wilf hopping about on one foot; I could hear Darren, Dad, Gran and Mum cheering. Then it dawned on me exactly what Rocky had done.

'He can run! Rocky can run!' I yelled and let out a great scream of joy.

Marcus scooped Wilf into the wheelchair and we ran across the park to join the others. Dad picked me up and swung me round.

'Happy birthday, Dad,' I said.

Dad couldn't speak; he just hugged me really tightly.

'Marcus!' said Mum, 'I knew you'd be part of the surprise!' She put her arms round him and gave him a kiss on the cheek.

'Thanks,' said Marcus. I expected him to be all embarrassed but he was grinning from ear to ear.

'And Wilf!' said Dad, shaking his hand. 'Great to see you out and about!'

'Told you that dog could run!' Wilf replied.

'And you were right,' said Dad, 'but however did you all keep it a secret?'

'It was ever so hard, Dad,' said Darren, 'especially when Mum guessed something was going on, so we had to …'

'That's a great story, love,' Mum butted in, 'so why don't you save it until Dad's had his birthday tea? You'll join us, won't you Wilf? It wouldn't be the same without you.'

'After all that hospital food? I wouldn't miss a proper meal for anything!' Wilf replied.

'Oh good,' said Gran, 'then I can tell you about that new Bingo club they've opened in town. There's a special offer for pensioners every Wednesday afternoon. Not that I'm nearly old enough to go, of course,' she added quickly.

Gran was flirting with Wilf! And, amazingly, it looked like he was enjoying it.

'Come on, everybody, I'm starving, and Rocky's ready for the biggest treat of his life,' said Dad.

Rocky trotted over and stood close to Dad, rubbing his head against Dad's knees and gazing up at him devotedly. Rocky looked so pleased with himself. He seemed different, too, somehow, but in a good way, like he'd discovered he was a proper greyhound once more.

'By the way Wilf, I'm amazed that matron let Anna and Marcus take you out on their own,' said Dad.

Marcus and I looked at each other. Wilf didn't say a word.

Mum turned to me. 'You did have permission to bring Wilf here, didn't you, Anna?' she asked.

That's when I heard a police siren approaching the other side of the park. It stopped suddenly and two policemen appeared. Mrs Appleby was with them and she was pointing in our direction. Then the three of them started running towards us.

Everyone stared at me.

'Anna?!' cried Mum and Dad at the same time.

There was going to be a lot of explaining to do, but I didn't care. Rocky was a winner again – and he wasn't the only one. We all were.

About the story

This story was inspired by a true dog: Rocky, a rescue greyhound, whose new owners gave him a loving home after his racing days were over.

Sadly, for many greyhounds there is no such happy ending. To find out what you can do to help, contact the Retired Greyhound Trust at *www.retiredgreyhounds. co.uk,* or telephone *0844 826 8424.*

Acknowledgements

I would like to thank all the people who helped me write this book. My Writers' Group: Valerie Bird, Vera Forster and Sandra Horn, were there from the very beginning, with their constant encouragement and guidance. Tim Gallop provided expert dog advice and invaluable comments on countless early drafts. Liz Redpath, of the Retired Greyhound Trust, Portsmouth, showed me round her kennels. Belinda Hollyer's feedback enabled me to make significant improvements. Niall Horn gave generously of his time and expertise to typeset my manuscript. Amanda Kent made the key suggestion.

Thank you also to Hilary Bowen, Hazel Dunn, Jade Dunn, Ursula Faulkner, Josian Gallop, Jean Giles, Jon Howell, Christy Kirkpatrick, Caroline Schade and Joanna Williams.

Finally, I would like to acknowledge the practical support and endorsement given to me by Ivor Stocker and the Retired Greyhound Trust, which made publication possible.

Greyhound facts

Did you know?

• Greyhounds are one of the oldest breeds of dogs and are known to have existed in Ancient Egypt.

• The greyhound is the only dog mentioned in the Bible.

• It is thought that the first greyhounds came to Britain with the Romans. Then, for hundreds of years, they were kept as hunting dogs.

• At first, only the most important people were allowed to own greyhounds, so they were called '**the dog of kings**'.

• Greyhounds can reach a top speed of 45 miles (over 72 kilometres) per hour. They can cover 500 metres in 30 seconds.

• Greyhound track racing began in Hendon, North London, in 1876.

Who are the
Retired Greyhound Trust?

Founded in 1976, the **Retired Greyhound Trust** cares and re-homes retired greyhounds.

For more than 30 years our nationwide army of volunteers have been finding loving homes for greyhounds (over 45,000 so far). We rescue needy greyhounds and take care of them until appropriate homes can be found. We are the National Charity which concentrates all its efforts on improving the lot of ex-racing greyhounds.

Why not look at our website:

www.retiredgreyhounds.co.uk

Charity no. 269668

Retired Greyhound Trust
2nd Floor, Park House
1-4 Park Terrace, Worcester Park
Surrey KT4 7JZ
Email: greyhounds@retiredgreyhounds.co.uk

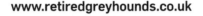

retired greyhound trust

191

ALSO PUBLISHED BY THE CLUCKET PRESS:

Two stories by Sandra Horn, illustrated by Karen Popham, set in the Lost Gardens of Heligan in Cornwall. For children aged 6-10,

- **THE MUD MAID** is a magical tale of how the Gardens came to be lost and found and restored to life and beauty once again. Hardcover isbn 978-0-9549256-1-1: Paperback isbn 978-0-9549256-0-4

- **THE GIANT.** There's a giant in the woods at the Lost Gardens of Heligan! He found his way there by travelling round the gardens. On his way, he came across all kinds of amazing things, including a pong, a putto, a scarecrow, some stripey buzzers, a hot seat and some spooks! You can see all the places he visited and follow his adventures, until at last you meet him in the spot he likes best of all. Paperback isbn 978-0-9549256-2-8

A new way to enjoy an old friend!

- **TATTYBOGLE - STORY AND MUSIC.** A cd audiobook of Sandra Horn's well-loved story read by the author, complemented by the enchanting songs written by Ruth Kenward for Tattybogle the Musical. isbn 978-0-9549256-4-2

For samples of the music, go to www.starshine.co.uk.

A story by Sandra Horn, illustrated by Mervyn Hathaway, set in Furzey Gardens in the New Forest.

- **THE FURZEY OAK.** Some of the oak trees in Furzey Gardens are a hundred years old or more. Their tall green crowns reach up towards the sky. On gusty days, the leaves whisper stories told by the wind. The oldest oak of all is hidden away. It bears no green leaves or acorns now, but it too has a story. Paperback isbn 978-0-9549256-5-9

A new edition of the favourite story by Sandra Horn, illustrated by Esther Connon.

- **THE MOON THIEVES**. The cat wants a dish of cream, the rat would like a whole blue cheese. Gran needs a silken pillow for her poor old head and the boy just wishes for a silver penny. Then one dark night, they look up and see a round white moon. They each think their dream has come true. Paperback isbn 978-0-9549256-6-6

*All publications are available from us at **www.tattybogle.com***